On My Own

"i love all the books cause they relate to my life in some way or another."—ABBIE

Who I Am

"It's so refreshing to read about the life of a Christian girl for once. I can't get enough!"— JAMEY LYNNE

"This is such an amazing, inspirational book and i have gotten so much out of it."—AMALIE

"This was so cool!! It actually helped me w/my real life!! I even prayed some of the prayers that she wrote down!"—HEATHER

"Wonderful! Another perfect book to go along with the first two."—DANI

"I really enjoyed it. When I read it, it made me realize my commitment to God was fading. Since then I have become rejuvenated and more committed."—ERICA

It's My Life

"This book inspired me to persevere through all my hardships and struggles, but it also brought me to the reality that even through my flaws, God can make Himself known in a powerful, life-changing way."—MEGHAN

"This book is unbelievable... It's so absolutely real to any teenage girl who is going through the tribulations of how to follow God. I've just recently found my path to God, and I can relate to Caitlin in many ways—it's a powerful thing."—EMILY

"I loved it!! It was so inspirational and even convicted me to have a stronger relationship with Christ. Thanks, Melody, this is the series I've been waiting for!!!"—SARAH

Becoming Me

"As I read this book, I laughed, cried, and smiled right along with Caitlin. It inspired me to keep my own journal. It changed my life forever. Thank you."—RACHEL

"I love all of the books! I could read them over and over!!!"—ASHLEY

"I couldn't put it down. When I was finished, I couldn't wait to get the second one!"—BETHANY

Diary of a Teenage Girl

Chloe Book Nº. 1

MY NAME IS CHLOE

a novel

MELODY CARLSON

Multnomah Books

MY NAME IS CHLOE

published by Multnomah Books

and in association with the literary agency of Sara A. Fortenberry

© 2002 by Melody Carlson

International Standard Book Number: 978-1-59052-018-5

Cover design by David Carlson Design
Cover photo by Photonica/Christian Roth/Spoon

Scripture quotations are from:

The Holy Bible, New International Version © 1973, 1984 by International Bible Society, used by permission of Zondervan Publishing House

Published in the United States by WaterBrook Multnomah, an imprint of the Crown Publishing Group, a division of Random House Inc., New York.

MULTNOMAH and its mountain colophon are registered trademarks of Random House Inc.

Printed in the United States of America

For information:
MULTNOMAH BOOKS
12265 ORACLE BOULEVARD, SUITE 200 • COLORADO SPRINGS, CO 80921

Library of Congress Cataloging-in-Publication Data
Carlson, Melody.
  My name is Chloe, by Chloe Miller : a novel / Melody Carlson.
    p. cm. -- (Diary of a teenage girl, Book no. 5)
  Summary: An intelligent but insecure fifteen-year-old aspiring musician, who sports off-beat clothes, spiked hair, and multiple piercings, questions the existence of God until she meets Him head-on in a graveyard.
  ISBN 1-59052-018-1 (Paperback)
  [1. Interpersonal relations--Fiction. 2. Conduct of life--Fiction. 3. Conversion--Fiction. 4. High schools--Fiction. 5. Schools--Fiction. 6. Diaries--Fiction.] I. Title.
PZ7 .C216637 My 2003
[Fic]--dc21

2002013132

09 10—12 11

BOOKS BY MELODY CARLSON:
Piercing Proverbs

DIARY OF A TEENAGE GIRL SERIES
Caitlin O'Conner:
Becoming Me

It's My Life

Who I Am

On My Own

I Do

Chloe Miller:
My Name Is Chloe

Sold Out

Road Trip

Face the Music

Kim Peterson:
Just Ask

Meant to Be

TRUE COLORS SERIES
Dark Blue, color me lonely

Deep Green, color me jealous

Torch Red, color me torn

Pitch Black, color me lost

One

Monday, September 2

I don't hate my life anymore. At least not today. I guess I consider myself a recovering pessimist. Or at least I'm trying. I used to be completely negative and cynical about everyone and everything, but I found that made it difficult to breathe. So now I'm trying to be more of a realist. That way I can be negative when I choose to, but there's still a little room for hope.

Some people think I am dark. I suppose they're a little frightened by me. By my appearance, or my opinions, or the way I look them straight in the eye without blinking or turning away, or even my music, which can be, I suppose, unsettling. Although I doubt they'd ever admit to such fears. Because no one likes to fess up to being scared. But I'll admit to it—at least within the privacy of my own journal. I seriously doubt that I'll go take out an ad in the Daily Times and go public with this news. Like anyone would care.

But it's true: I am scared. And sometimes I scare myself. Okay, I'm not talking about when I look in the mirror, although that can be a little frightening, especially on those mornings when I have flattened down bed head and my eyelashes are stuck together with that gluck that gathers in your eyes while you're asleep. But for the most part it's not my appearance that scares me. Although I'm sure I seem frightening to some people—narrow-minded people who want everyone to look the same—like cookie-cutter characters where everyone has a happy face stamped right into their heads.

I've seen people stare at my hair (I cut it myself— all jaggedy so it can stick out in all sorts of interesting shapes, and I like putting colors on it, such as magenta and lime and purple), and I've seen some people stare at my multiple-pierced ears and belly button and wince or just back away. As if this is something unusual. And I suppose I derive some weird sense of satisfaction from their response. Like, see "I told you so." Does that make sense?

My friend Caitlin O'Conner (about the straightest chick I know) says I use my appearance to keep people from getting too close to me. And maybe she's right, although I've never admitted this to anyone before, except her and then only briefly. But I do sort of enjoy keeping up an exterior that turns some people off—or even frightens them. I figure if they're so shallow that they're threatened by my appearance, well, then who wants to know them anyway?

Besides, if you don't let people get close to you, you lessen your chances of getting hurt by them. Right? And that's something I could sure live without. Not that I'm afraid of pain, because I'm not. Believe me, I'm not! I just don't go around inviting it to come over to visit me on a regular basis.

I guess that's one thing that scares me though—the way I keep shoving people away from me. It's as if it's become this habit that's getting harder and harder to break. In fact, I've gotten uncomfortably comfortable with my isolation. Well, for the most part. I mean, no one really wants to be alone all the time. Do they? But somehow Caitlin just pushed her way past all my barbed-wire barriers and brick walls and actually became my friend. Well, sort of. Actually, I still wonder if she reached out to me because my brother Josh told her I was such a pathetic mess. She probably felt sorry for me too, because she's that kind of person—overly caring and sympathetic—something she needs to be careful of, I think. Too much empathy can get you into trouble.

But besides Josh's involvement, I suspect Caitlin (a Christian who takes her faith real seriously) probably had great hopes of converting me, not that I've ever done anything to encourage her. But that's all history now because Caitlin has just gone off to college. And I'm sure she'll forget all about me before long, if she hasn't already. I guess it just proves my point about not getting too close to people. Because in the long run, whether they mean to or not, they'll eventually hurt you or leave. That's what I've found to be true anyway.

But here's another thing that scares me about myself: It's the way I question just about everything. My parents call me rebellious and headstrong. My teachers say I have an attitude problem. Caitlin just says I'm searching. And in some ways I think she's closer to the truth than the rest of them. But for whatever reason, it seems as though nothing ever comes easily for me.

I'm not like Josh, the golden boy, who just seems to coast through life on his wave of charm, good looks, and general popularity. I'm probably more like my older brother Caleb, although since he left home while I was in grade school, it seems I barely knew him. But his life has been pretty messy too. Actually he's done a much worse job of it than I have (so far). I realize that could change for me any day now. And according to my parents it will.

They're predicting that I'll seriously blow it in my first year of high school. They could be right. I just might blow it—or blow up. I might explode into millions of tiny pieces and fly throughout the universe. Or maybe I'll try to prove them wrong. I'm still not sure which way this thing will go.

Caitlin thinks I'm going to do "something wonderful with my life." Ha! But then she's like that—the perennial Pollyanna of the new millennium. And I'll admit I liked that book as a child, back when I thought everything always ended up "happily ever after." I just don't believe that anymore. And I don't mean to slam her exactly, but I do think she's a little too idealistic. I mean, what could I possibly do that would ever be described as "wonderful"? I don't even like that word! Like I said, I'm trying to lean more toward realism, even if it does get me down sometimes.

And I suppose that's why I question God a lot. But that's only on the days when I still believe in him. Because a lot of times I don't. A lot of times I wonder about things like religious wars and starvation and child slavery and just general greed and cruelty—and I find it hard to believe that God would allow such chaos.

But Caitlin says it's okay to question God. She says, "He can handle it." And she positively assured me that no matter what questions I ask, God has all the answers. But she also said that I might not always like all his answers. But what probably frightens me the most is the very

likely possibility that he won't answer at all—
the possibility that he's not even there—and
that we're all alone on this rapidly spinning
ball called earth going nowhere fast. And for
some reason that scares me more than anything.
But I'd never admit this to anyone. In a way it
seems pretty childish to see it written down. It's
as if I try to act all grown up and mature and, I
suppose, even tough, but inside I'm just a
frightened little kid. Pretty scary, huh?

There we have it. I have just confessed my
biggest fears, but I have some smaller ones too.
They may seem minor compared to what I've just
written above, but unfortunately they don't feel
minor right now. I'll tell you what my most cur-
rent pressing fear is: School starts tomorrow.

It's my first year in high school, and I don't
even have one single friend to walk onto campus
with. Oh, sure, it's my own fault since I no longer
act, talk, or dress like my old friends. But were
they really my friends? Would real friends shun
me so easily? I think Jessie and I might've eventually become friends again, but then she moved
last spring.

But to think I lost all this on account of a
moronic boyfriend who stabbed me in the back
because I wouldn't give in to him? How stupid is
that? Maybe it was one of those Freudian things,
like I really wanted to blow my life into

smithereens on purpose. Or not. The fact is, I now have to face entering high school as a solo act. And that freaks me out.

Pitiful, isn't it? Oh, I keep telling myself that I'll just act exceptionally hard and aloof, dressed in my tough chick threads (which have sent my mom to her room with a headache again), and I'll march right in there and take nothing from nobody. But despite my plan, I still feel pretty worried. And a small part of me wishes I'd listened to my mom and gotten some of those more "mainstream" kinds of clothes and tried to make what she calls a "fresh start."

I suppose this is where my rebelliousness comes into play. I just could NOT do it. I could NOT give in to my mom. I think it's because I actually like how I look. It's kind of creative, you know, like an alternative rock star. And so far I only have seven piercings, and I think I'll keep it at that since seven is a perfect number. And I don't even have a tattoo (although I've been tempted a time or two and am still considering trying a henna one). You'd think that alone would make my mom happy.

And I like how my hair looks all spiky and wild and colorful. Really, I think I look pretty cool. And since I AM a serious and aspiring musician, I think this image works for me. Of course, no one (well, except for Caitlin) really knows how committed I am to my music. Maybe I'll get more out there with it this year. Maybe I'll see if I can play at the new coffeehouse that just came to town. Who knows? I could even become famous someday. It happens.

I've heard of fifteen-year-olds who've hit it big. Besides, everyone thinks I'm old for my age, plus I'm old in my class since my parents started me to school a year late due to a silly childhood illness that didn't seem like such a big deal at the time, to me anyway. Even my grandmother says I have the soul of an old woman, although I don't think she necessarily thinks that's a good thing. But maybe that's why I've always related better to older people. The kids in my own grade feel too immature for me, and yet I still feel like a little kid sometimes too.

Caitlin encouraged me to journal down my thoughts. She said it's a good way to get in touch with my feelings, although I feel pretty in touch already—sometimes too much so. She also said I should write down prayers. I tried not to laugh when she said that, but I'm thinking: What prayers? I mean, I don't ever pray. I don't even want to pray. And why is that? I say I still believe in God. Well, sometimes anyway. So why wouldn't I want to try praying to him?

I guess it's because I'm worried that, if he really does exist, he'll want to change me. And

I'm not sure I'm ready for that yet. Even though I'm unhappy and mixed up and feeling a little frightened, I'm still not sure I want to change. So instead of a prayer, I guess I'll just write down a poem. Because I'm not only a musician, I'm also a poet. And I am me! Chloe.

WHAT IF
what if all there is
is me?
what if i am all i see?
what if life is only this?
and ignorance is bliss?
what if love is only pain?
and nothing can be gained
by living every day
and there is no better way?
what then?
cm

TWO

Friday, September 6

This was the longest week of my life. Every single day was grueling—worse torture than walking barefoot over thumbtacks or having bamboo slivers stabbed beneath your fingernails. I am utterly exhausted. Now, for whatever reason, I have promised myself not to swear or cuss or use profanity in my diary. (I also try to avoid such cheap tactics in my lyrics.) But right now I could easily back down on this puritanical pledge.

Because what I want to know is: What's the bleeping reason for throwing a bunch of insecure, heartless, narcissistic, shallow, malicious, crass, and did I mention self-centered, adolescents together into one huge merciless cement complex and making them spend four years of their young impressionable lives together in there? If we were rats we'd probably start chewing off each other's tails by the third day. Come to think of it, that's exactly what a lot of kids do. But what's the point of this pubescent penitentiary? Is it because the rest of the world is so frightened of teenagers that they want to keep us off the streets for at least seven hours a day, five days a week, and nine months out of the year—like a part-time prison? Because it makes absolutely no sense to me.

Like today. I'm just minding my own business, washing my hands at the sink in the girls' bathroom (a dangerous practice, I have learned, much more hazardous than walking around with toilet germs) when Tiffany Knight looks over at me and says, "Hey, I thought Goth went out with the last millennium." Then she and her moronic friends laugh as if that's real funny. Now I've known Tiffany since junior high, and she's always been a great big pain in the you-know-what.

She's one of those girls who craves, more than anything, to be really popular, but she can never quite make it into the inner circle of the elite. Probably because she's so mean. As a result she's gathered a small group of friends (Tiffany wannabes) that she controls like a bunch of trained monkeys. And her group of followers seems to derive a twisted pleasure from torturing anyone they perceive as below them—which probably consists of most of the rest of us.

Okay, I realize now that my first mistake was to even talk with her. I should've just walked away. But regrettably I reacted. Remember how I like to learn things the hard way?

"Do you even know what Goth is?" I ask, but not

in a mean way exactly. At least I didn't think so at the time.

Well, this stops her for a moment, as she stares at me with obvious disdain and a pretense of superiority, but it doesn't shut her up long enough for me to make my exit. Besides that, she and her goons are now blocking the door. So she sticks her chin out and says, "I know that your look is definitely the lamest thing I've seen since my grandma's old Persian cat got his head stuck in the garbage disposal."

Now this really cracks her friends up, but I don't quite see the humor. Still, instead of just walking away, I toss back my own zinger. "Well, Tiffany, I guess you should know since you and your cookie-cutter friends all look like a bad day at the Fashion Butterfly." Now that's a pretty good put-down because Fashion Butterfly is this old ladies' store on Main Street where no self-respecting teenager would ever be seen. My mom won't even go in there.

Naturally no one laughs at my joke. And the next thing I know, Tiffany is right in my face, so close I can actually smell her Tommy Hilfiger perfume as well as see a fairly large but well-concealed zit on the tip of her nose. And her friends are right behind her.

"You think you're pretty tough, don't you, Chloe?" Tiffany's breath smells like that sorry excuse for pizza the cafeteria dishes up twice a week.

Well, as much as I don't want to experience any physical pain or discomfort, I also have no desire to give up my tough-girl image either. I mean, sometimes being tough is about all a girl has. So I stand firm and say, "I'm sure you think you're pretty tough too, Tiffany. At least when you've got your goons to back you up." Then I actually take what I hope is an intimidating step closer to her and we are literally nose-to-nose (an experience I'd just as soon forget—and soon). "I wonder how tough you'd be if it were just you and me."

In that same instant I am exceedingly thankful for my additional few inches of height as well as the fact that I am wearing my studded black leather bracelet, not to mention my sturdy Doc Martens boots. But at the same time my heart is literally running the hundred-yard dash, and I want to disappear in a vapor of purple haze. Because, despite my tough appearance, I am basically a nonviolent person.

Just then, I hear the door open and I glance past Tiffany and her friendly thugs to see Laura Mitchell walk in. Now all I know about Laura is that she sits behind me in choir and has a pretty decent voice—in fact, she's really quite good. But we've never had an actual conversation before today.

"What's up?" she asks loudly, pushing her way past the cookie-cutter girls clogging the doorway. "You staging a fight in here or something?" She eyes me curiously then turns her attention to Tiffany. "Maybe I should go out in the hallway and announce to everyone that there's going be a big cat fight in here. I'm sure they'd love to see you all scratching and screaming and pulling out hair—"

"Back off!" Tiffany hisses. Her attention has moved from me and is fully on Laura now.

"Hey..." Laura holds up her hands then lifts her brows as if she wants to remain neutral. "I just came in here to—"

"Why don't you just take a hike, sistah?"

Now I didn't mention that Laura is of African-American descent, but she definitely does not appear to appreciate Tiffany's snide little sistah remark. And the next thing I know Laura squeezes in next to me, positioning herself directly in front of Tiffany. Then she narrows her eyes and speaks in a quiet but intense voice. "I am not your sister."

Just as I'm bracing myself for everything ugly to break loose, the door opens again and Mrs. Langford, an elderly English teacher, walks in and looks curiously at our little throng. "Everything all right in here, girls?" she asks in her apple-pie voice.

This mercifully breaks the happy party up, and Tiffany and her monkeys slip out the door acting like the good little girls they want everyone to think they are. Everyone except for us unlucky ones—the ones they set their sights on—to search out and destroy. That always includes any of us who are willing to look or act or even think different. Because difference is not tolerated by people like Tiffany.

Laura and I spoke only briefly in the bathroom. I think I was more shaken than I wanted to admit. Besides, Mrs. Langford was probably listening from behind the stall door. I'm not sure what made her use the girls' bathroom in the first place, since they have a special one for teachers, but maybe it was occupied. Just the same, I'm glad she did. And I promised myself that I'd put out more of an effort in my composition class with her.

"See ya 'round," I said to Laura as I left.

She nodded. "Yeah, take it easy."

And so I'm thinking, maybe I should try to get to know this girl better. But at the same time, I'm wondering why she'd want to know me. She seems to have a big group of friends already. And to be honest, they look a little too preppy for me. Okay, not as bad as Tiffany and her wannabes. But they definitely seem to be into labels and fashion and image and could be shallow. Although I could be

all wrong too since I don't really know them personally. They're from a different middle school,
and they seem pretty tight-knit. They probably
have no interest in hanging with a white chick
anyway. Besides, I'm sure they think I'm pretty
weird. And that's okay. I'm used to being alone.
And I'm pretty good at acting as if I like it.

SAFETY IN NUMBERS
is there really safety in numbers
like telephone numbers?
or address numbers?
or IQ numbers?
or whole numbers like 3 or 5 or 7 or 101?
which number is the safest?
and what about the number one
which, like the cheese, stands alone?
alone, lone, lonely—all divisible by one
so do you know my number?
it's easy to recall
it's easy to remember
you wanna give me a call?
cm

Sunday, September 8

Had a big fight with Mom tonight. What a surprise. She's been on my case all week to clean up
my room. But I think, hey, it's my room. If I want

to live like a pig, well, who's it gonna hurt?

"It's just like your life," she said as she blocked my doorway so I couldn't close it and couldn't leave unless I wanted to jump out the window, which I only try to do when my parents aren't looking.

"Yeah, well, it's my life, isn't it?" I flopped down on my bed and stared at the ceiling, wishing she would just go away. These little confrontations don't help anything. And my mom has this tendency to let things go for a long time, but then like a pot that's been left on the stove too long, she boils over and burns whoever crosses her path. Usually, my dad intervenes about that time, but he was out of town on business.

"You live under our roof! And you are our daughter! You might think you're all grown up, but you're still a child, and there are certain things you have to do!"

"Duh."

"Are you listening to me, Chloe?"

"How could I not be?" I sat up and looked at her. "You're screaming so loud I'm sure everyone in our neighborhood is listening."

Now this quieted her down a couple of decibels because despite everything else, she does care what the neighbors think. A lot.

"Look, Chloe," she was softening now. "I try to be patient with you. I put up with your clothes, your hair, and your attitude, but there are some things I simply cannot put up with."

"Such as?"

"Your room, for instance. I insist that you clean it at least once a week. It's a—a health hazard. Look at the cereal bowl over there." She pointed to a bowl on my dresser. "It's turning green."

"It's a science experiment."

"Chloe!"

"Yeah, yeah. Okay, maybe I could clean up a little. But why do you have to come so unglued about such minor things?"

Okay, that was probably a mistake. My mom took that as some sort of an invitation to really bare her soul to me. Something I could've easily lived without tonight.

But being a somewhat dutiful although somewhat detached parent, she came over and sat on my bed. "It's because I'm worried about you, Chloe."

"Well, don't be."

"I can't help it. You're my daughter. And you don't seem happy to me."

"Happy?" I laughed sarcastically. "Is there any such thing?"

"Of course, there is. Lots of people are happy. Your father and I are happy. Josh is happy."

I noticed she didn't include Caleb on her little happy list, but thinking better of it, I didn't mention it either. "Well, did it ever occur to you that some of us just aren't _meant_ to be happy?"

"But you used to be happy. At least I thought you were. You had friends and you went to slumber parties and you played soccer and acted, well, like a normal girl—"

I socked my pillow with my fist. "So that's it. You want me to be a _normal_ girl. You want me to dress and act and talk and think just like the rest of the superficial airhead girls that go to my creeped-out school. They're all clawing and climbing to be among the elite, the best, the queens of the high school ball, willing to walk all over anyone who gets in their way as they fight their way to the top. That is, if they even can get to the top, and most can't. You want me to be like _that?_"

Her eyebrows shot up and she pressed her lips together.

"That's really it, isn't it?" My voice was loud now. "You simply cannot stand that I'm not like that. That I'm not like you!"

"Oh, Chloe, I'm glad that you are your own individual—"

"No, you're not, Mom! You wish and you probably even pray that I would be just like the others—what you call _happy!_ If you could, you'd probably clone me into the spitting image of yourself back when you were in high school—

Miss Rah-Rah Rally and Homecoming Queen. Well, you better get over it, Mom, 'cause it just ain't gonna happen!"

Now I could see her getting all weepy—the second act of her annual "Be Like Everyone Else" show. "You're just going through a difficult time—"

"You got that one right. Life is difficult. And high school is the pits."

"But things can change—"

"Don't count on it, Mom. At least not if you're thinking it's me who's going to do the changing. Because, like it or not, I am who I am."

"But you're unhappy."

Despite myself I let a cuss word fly. But my mom just continued, pretending not to even notice. "I just want you to be happy, Chloe."

If I heard that happy word one more time tonight, I might literally explode—go flying into a thousand pieces, splattering all over my room in a nasty bloody mess.

"Honey?" I could feel her looking at me now, and I swear I knew what she was about to ask. "You—uh—you're not involved in drugs, are you?"

I sighed deeply and shook my head. Here we go again. "First of all, Mom, if I was doing drugs, do you really think I'd tell you?"

She shrugged. "I don't know. But we're supposed to ask."

"Secondly, I'm not. Not that I don't consider it occasionally—like when people push me too hard to be happy. I mean, maybe it would be some kind of escape from all this—"

"Oh no, Chloe, it would only—"

"Yeah, yeah, I know. 'It would only mess me up even more.' I've heard the speeches. I saw what happened to Caleb. And I'm not really into self-destruction. Not today anyway. But you might check with me next week, Mom. Maybe on Thursday. Right now I have homework to do. And then, of course, I _must_ clean my room."

She stood and smoothed down her Liz Claiborne pants, every pleat in perfect place. "Okay, then. I'm glad we had this talk, dear."

I tried to hide my exasperation. "Yeah, me too."

Then I did my homework. But instead of cleaning my room, I've been sitting here venting into my diary. And now it's late. Sorry, Mom, guess my room will have to wait. Besides, it's not so bad, really. I mean, I can still make it from my bed to the door without tripping—if I'm careful. And tomorrow I might go through and take out all the rotting food items. That should make her feel better.

ROTTEN CHEERIOS
green little circles
adhered to a bowl

rejected, dejected, subject to decay
once soggy and wet
now rotting away
but oh you are changing
growing fuzzy and green
yet no appreciation
will ever be seen
for you are so worthless
so sorry so sad
you rotten old cheerios
you are very bad
now get outta my room!
cm

Thursday, September 12

Being alone makes you think more. But sometimes too much thinking makes you feel as though you're going crazy. But if you _think_ you're going crazy, maybe you're not—since they always say the crazy ones are the last ones to know. But I'm not so sure about that.

I think I miss having Caitlin around. As Pollyanna-like as she is and as much as I dislike those perfect girls with their sugary smiles, Caitlin was sort of like good medicine to me. Usually after spending time with her, I would try harder to be a better person. I know that sounds completely moronic, but it's the truth.

Today a guy came up to me and offered me some speed. I can't even remember exactly how I responded, probably something like, "Hey, I'm going about as fast as I want to at the moment."

And he just smiled and said, "Cool." Then he introduced himself and we talked for a while. His name was Spencer Abbott and he seemed like a pretty nice guy, really. Oh, I know how some people think that anyone who takes drugs is really messed up and dangerous. But mostly I think they're just searching, like me. At least I think of myself as a searcher. The problem is, I don't seem to be finding whatever it is I'm looking for. Or maybe I'm just not sure what it is I'm looking for or where to even look.

If I were to be perfectly honest—and that's what I'm trying to do in this diary. If you can't be honest with your diary then who can you be honest with?—I suppose I'm looking for love. Oh wow. It's not easy to write that down. First of all it sounds so completely cliché, and on top of that, it's so lame and pitiful—all things I despise. It hurts my head to even read those words. But that, I think, is the sad ugly truth: Chloe Miller is looking for love. Barf!

So does this mean I think my parents don't love me? No, I'm sure they do—in their own impaired way—but their love often seems dependent on me meeting their HIGH expectations. And unfortunately, I seem to do that less and less. Mostly it feels as though they ignore me or simply tolerate me—and then just barely. As if they're counting the days until I finally grow up and graduate from high school and get outta their picture-perfect lives. That might be an unfair judgment on my part, but it's just how I feel.

So am I looking for the love of a boyfriend? Someone to wrap his arms around me and pull me close and whisper sweet secrets in my ear? Well, maybe. Unfortunately, other than Spencer (who's not bad looking) no one seems to be beating down my door. Would I get involved with Spencer? I'm not sure. And since I'm feeling desperate, who knows? But it would bother me that he's so into drugs. And he is; I can tell. And I guess I'd be worried that I might get caught up in that world too—purely by association. I just don't think I'm ready for that.

So what is it then? Maybe I just need a good friend or two. Someone who understands and accepts me—someone I can talk to. Caitlin was a little like that, but in some ways she always seemed "above" me. Not that she was snooty. Because despite that she hung with the cool crowd, like my brother, she was actually nice. Maybe the problem is that she's so much older. And, yes, because she seems so perfect. Impossibly and impeccably perfect.

Oh, I know how she tells me about her flaws and her mistakes and regrets. Like yesterday, she e-mailed me about her horrible roommate in college, saying how she'd really like to just drop-kick her over the nearest goalpost, etc.— well, you get the picture. So, I suppose Caitlin's not so perfect. But then she's not here, either.

It has occurred to me—for some reason a lot this week—that I could try talking to God. (That's what Caitlin calls it. She hardly ever says "praying" even though I know that's what she means. But she calls it "talking to God.") Still, like I've already said, this just feels really weird to me. And for a long time, I've had some sort of very real blockade that I can't seem to get around. But now I find myself thinking about it—almost daily. But still I haven't done it. I'm not sure that I even can. I mean, exactly how do you start something like that anyway? Do you just say, "Hey, God, I wanna talk?" It sounds so strange, demented even. And did I mention crazy? So maybe I am losing it. Maybe that's just where I'm heading these days.

OFF TO CRAZYVILLE
there she goes again
off to crazyville
with her red balloon
and a fat baboon

she talks to herself
and says she talks to god
and that he's listening
but all she really hears
is the ringing in her ears
and the singing in her brain
as she walks out in the rain
with no shoes on
there she goes again
off to crazyville
cm

Three

Saturday, September 14

Okay, here's the latest weird flash. Chloe Miller is talking to God! Is she crazy? Losing her mind? I'm not sure, but here I am starting to write about myself in third person. That's probably not so good either. Okay, chill, girl. Just chill.

It all started yesterday—on Friday the thirteenth even—I should've known better than to go to school on such an unlucky day. But I did. For at least half the day anyway. I ended up skipping the second half. Hey, I didn't say I had suddenly become perfect or even a Christian—I only said that I've taken up talking to God. And I suspect he may not even like what I'm saying to him because frankly, he hasn't talked back. But I suppose I didn't expect him to. Not really. The surprising thing is that I'm still doing it.

I went to school yesterday telling myself to be thankful that it was Friday and I'd have two whole days to recover from a seriously deranged week. I'll spare you the details except to say that Tiffany Knight has targeted me for her whipping girl. She hardly allows a day to pass without some lame attempt at making my life miserable—as if I need any help in that particular area! But I was just minding my own business, thinking about a new song I'm working on and whether I have enough nerve to take my homemade audiocassette down to the new coffeehouse in town. Or maybe I should just see if I could get up there on that little stage and read a poem for starters. I'm still not sure. Isn't it ironic that I try to escape such abuse and public humiliation at school, but then I'm willing to climb onto a live stage and actually invite even more? Sometimes I astound myself.

But back to Tiffany. It was fourth period, choir, and Mr. Thompson had just asked anyone who was interested in auditioning for a small girls' ensemble (to start rehearsing some special songs for the Christmas concert) to stay afterward. Naturally, I stayed. So did Laura. And to my disappointment, Tiffany and several of her monkeys stayed as well.

Hey, it's a free world, I told myself. Although I've never heard Tiffany sing, since she's in the first soprano section and I'm in second soprano (although I can sing anything between alto and soprano). Still I couldn't imagine how anyone as mean as Tiffany could possibly have a voice worth listening to.

So, I nonchalantly moved down to the front

row, where we were supposed to wait our turns, and began doodling in my notebook. One by one the girls stepped up and sang a few bars from a song we're working on right now called "The Falling Leaves." Most of them were acting pretty self-conscious and seemed embarrassed about singing solo, and some were really messing up badly. Each time someone squeaked or hit a wrong note, Tiffany and her cohorts would break into giggles. Mr. Thompson warned them to be quiet, and I even tossed them a dark look. Okay, that was a mistake.

But I was relieved when Mr. Thompson called on Tiffany next. I think he figured this was one way to shut them up. Well, Tiffany strutted down to the piano like she was the queen of the choir and started to sing. And I have to admit she was okay, but nothing to be particularly proud about. But when she returned to her seat, she looked at me as if to say, "Top that." I just rolled my eyes and went back to doodling. Her three friends sang next, and one was okay but the other two were pretty hopeless.

Then Laura was called down, and I quit doodling and smiled at her as she took her place by the piano. I think she saw me too. And then she sang with a boldness and confidence that was totally cool. I started clapping as soon as she finished, and a number of other girls joined in.

But of course not Tiffany and her monkeys.

Then it was my turn. Emboldened by Laura's brave performance, I went down there and gave it my best shot too. And once again, applause followed. Mr. Thompson smiled and said, "That was great, Chloe." And I felt pretty sure that I'd be picked. About that time I noticed Tiffany and her tribe getting up to leave.

"I'm hungry," said Tiffany. "And my ears are starting to hurt." I'm sure she was aiming this one at me, or maybe Laura. But bolstered by the applause and Mr. Thompson's praise, I ignored her, staying behind to listen to the rest of the girls try out. And from then on out we clapped for everyone regardless of her performance.

"Good job, girls," said Mr. Thompson as he closed the piano. "I'll post the results on my office door, right after lunch." Then as I was about to leave, he said, "Chloe, can I see you a minute?"

"Sure." I walked back over. "What's up?"

He smiled again. "You really have a fantastic voice. And I'm curious about how comfortable you'd be doing solos now and then?"

I grinned. "Are you kidding? I'd love to. Music is my life."

"I thought so. Well, great then. I won't keep you from missing all of lunch."

So feeling as if I'd just won the lottery—or better yet a Grammy—I headed off toward the cafeteria, even though I didn't feel hungry. But just as I turned the corner, I saw them: Tiffany and her thugs. I thought maybe I was overreacting at first, because I felt certain they were waiting for me. But then I countered that thought, thinking I was just being ridiculously paranoid—I mean, what were they going to do? Mug me for my lunch money? It's a shame I didn't go with my original instincts because I could've made a getaway if I'd tried. But I didn't. Instead, I just kept walking.

"I don't know what makes you think you're so hot," said Tiffany, coming right up beside me. Then she gave me a sharp shove.

"Hey!" I yelled, hoping someone down the next hall might hear me.

Then Tiffany's friend Kerry pushed me from the other side. "You think you're so tough!" she snarled in my face. And then in a blur that I can't even completely remember—it was like a scene from a bad teen flick—the four of them had me up against the lockers. I can still feel the indentation of the lock imprinted into my spine.

"You are a loser, Miller!" Tiffany slapped me across the face.

"Yeah," echoed Kerry, and then she actually punched me in the stomach.

I just glared at them, hating them all like I've never hated anyone or anything before. I even tasted the hate, or maybe it was just the blood from where my lip was cut, but it tasted like metal and it felt like pure hate.

"You're a total misfit!" said Tiffany. "And this school would be better off without lowlifes like you slumming it up." She gave me another hard shove, banging my head against the locker with a loud bang. They all backed away, laughing hysterically like a pack of hyenas. Then they ran out the door that led to the courtyard. I just stood there fighting back tears of rage.

Then I turned around and kicked the locker with my Doc Marten, and the sound echoed throughout the hallway, maybe throughout the entire school. Why hadn't I thought to kick them or to defend myself? Why had I just stood there and allowed them to beat on me like that?

I marched over to the emergency exit, knowing full well that I would set off the alarm, and I walked out of there. Then I ran. I left that school determined to NEVER go back there again. Not ever! And for the first time I could actually understand why our school has a metal detector. Because right then and there, I felt certain that if for some reason I was forced to return, I would come back armed and ready to defend myself. And a life sentence in prison seemed like a small price to pay. At least I figured I might be in a cell all by myself.

A normal person would probably wonder if I told anyone about this little altercation—like my parents or someone at school or even the police. But what good would it really do? Naturally, Tiffany and her thugs would deny it. It would be their word against mine. And they look so sweet and innocent and "normal" in their little designer-of-the-week outfits. And of course I look like, well, like me. Besides, no one witnessed the crime.

Oh, maybe if I'd had a really good friend, I would've told her. But I strongly suspected it would do no good to tattle, and it would probably just increase my troubles. And as much as I hate those girls and as much as I wish they could get what they deserve (severe punishment and justice), I know that there's nothing I can do to make this happen. And I suppose that makes me feel pretty helpless.

Perhaps that's the reason I found myself finally, after all this resistance, actually talking to God. After ditching school, I walked all the way across town to the cemetery. I like to go there sometimes to think and to write poetry and songs. I know it's weird so it's not something I've ever told anyone about. But it's quiet there and my mind can breathe.

Once I got there, I went straight to my favorite gravesite (in the old section) and sat by a headstone that reads: "Katherine Lucinda McCall,

born June 11, 1880, died December 21, 1901. May
she dance with the angels." For some reason I
liked that part about dancing with the angels. I
don't even know why. But it disturbed me that
Katherine died just before Christmas, and when
she was only twenty-one, just entering adult-
hood. And I've even written a song (a ballad
really) about her life (as I imagine it anyway).

But there I was, just sitting there (not really
thinking about Katherine) and feeling more down
than I've ever felt before, when I looked up at the
sky and thought: I feel like a piece of crud stuck
to the bottom of God's shoe.

And then I said, "So, why don't you just wipe me
off and get it over with?"—my first words to God
since those grade-school days of reciting rhyming
prayers from Sunday school. Pretty weird, huh?
And then, as if something in me had just been
unlocked, I kept on talking. Asking God all sorts
of impossible and rebellious and irreverent questions. Like "Why do you let people like Tiffany
Knight and her friends even breathe the air?" And
"Why is this world so messed up that innocent
children all over the globe are dying of AIDS and
hunger and being used for pornography or prostitution?" And "Why does it hurt so much to be
alive?" And "Did you really make me? And if you
did, what could you have possibly been thinking?"
And "Are you really even listening to me? Are you

really there?" Stuff like that. And while I'm not exactly proud of the way I spoke to God, I'm thinking it's better than nothing. Maybe it's a start.

But here's what's got me thinking. I felt better afterward. Oh, I didn't feel good or happy or like I could forgive and forget Tiffany and her monkeys. But somehow I felt better. Then I walked home and ate a peanut butter and jelly sandwich and drank a tall glass of milk (my own personal form of comfort food). And then I went to bed and slept until noon today. I guess I was tired. Here's the poem I wrote yesterday, after I first spoke to God, before I came home from the graveyard.

LOOKING FOR GOD
can you see him, Katherine Lucinda
as you dance with your angel friends up above?
can you hear him, Katherine Lucinda
can you look in his eyes and feel his love?
because i am looking
looking for him
in all the wrong places
where chances are slim
looking for god
when i don't even know
if he exists
if he will show
but i won't give in
to the hope i can't share

> to think that he listens
> to think that he cares
> because i've no faith
> and i'm stuck to his heel
> like dirty, old gum
> hey, god, are you real?
> cm

Monday, September 16

Well, despite swearing I'd never return, I went back to school today. And incredibly, it wasn't too bad. In fact, I almost think that Tiffany and her monkeys are feeling a little scared or guilty or something. But other than a dark glance from Tiffany during choir, none of them gave me any grief all day.

And I won't waste any more diary time on them. Because something good happened. I saw Laura in the hall between first and second period, and I went over and asked if she'd seen the list last Friday for the small ensemble group.

"Didn't you see it?"

"No, I—uh—had to leave."

She looked slightly suspicious but then seemed to dismiss it. "Well, congratulations. You made it."

"I'm sure you made it too."

"But guess who didn't?"

I shrugged.

"Tiffany Knight <u>didn't</u> make the cut." She glanced over her shoulder. "And neither did her friends."

"Well, you've just made my day."

She laughed. "You got that right."

Then after choir, Laura caught up with me in the hall outside the lunchroom. "You know, you've really got a good voice, Chloe."

"Thanks, but so do you."

"Well, I was just wondering if you do any other kind of music."

By the way Laura twisted the strap to her backpack, I realized that she was probably uncomfortable talking to me. Had I done anything to make her feel that way? So I smiled and said, "Yeah, I play guitar and piano and I like to write my own songs."

"Really?" Her eyes lit up. "I play bass."

"You're kidding? You play bass? How'd you get into that?"

"It's my brother's fault. He took it up a few years ago, even played with a band. He talked my mom into getting him all this stuff, then after a while he just gave it up. Before she had a chance to sell anything, I took it up myself."

"Wow, maybe we can jam together sometime."

"Yeah, that'd be cool."

About that time some of Laura's friends were

coming up and, it seemed, eyeing me with curiosity or maybe even suspicion. Suddenly I felt as if I'd intruded into their space. "Well, I better go."

"See ya, Chloe," She turned to join her friends. They laughed and joked with her as if they were some exclusive society. And I must admit I felt jealous.

It seems everyone has a clique to belong to. I looked over to where Spencer and some of his friends were hanging. I suspected I'd be welcome there, but then I also knew they're into drugs—at least he is—and that often means the rest are too. But somehow, in that instant, I just felt too lonely to care. Besides, I didn't have any intention of snorting a line of coke right there in the lunchroom, or anywhere else for that matter. So I grabbed my regular salad and soda and went over to their table. "Mind if I join you?"

"That's cool," said Spencer, scooting over to make room.

"I'm Chloe," I announced as I opened the dressing and squeezed it over my salad.

"Seen you around," said a redheaded guy across the table. He had a tattoo of a dragon on his right arm and a pair of lip rings, one on each side, kind of like fangs. "I'm Jake."

"Hey, Jake." I smiled and took a bite of salad.

"I'm Allie," said the small blond girl sitting next to him.

I studied her for a minute. "Did we go to middle school together?"

"Just during sixth grade," she answered. "Then my folks moved out of state. They just moved back last summer. And now it's like no one even remembers me." She laughed. "Or at least they pretend not to."

"I remember you. We had art together and you were really good."

She smiled. "Thanks."

"Do you still do art?"

"Yeah, I try." Then she peered more closely at me. "But you've changed. Didn't you used to be one of those preppy chicks?"

Now I laughed. "Maybe, it's hard to remember that far back. But I guess I got sick of the hypocrisy and decided to try just being myself for a change."

"Cool," said Spencer. That seems to be his favorite word.

"_You_ used to be a preppy?" said a guy who'd been quiet until now. And I must admit I'd been observing him from the corner of my eye. His dark Latino looks were definitely attractive, and I liked how his thick, black hair was pulled back in a ponytail—very sophisticated.

"That's Cesar," said Allie. "He _hates_ preppies."

"Not totally." Cesar stared at me. "It's just hard to imagine _you_ as a preppy."

"Hey, it's not something I'm especially proud of. It's sort of a family curse, if you know what I mean."

He laughed. "Yeah, like everyone assumes I speak Spanish."

So I sat there and chatted with these kids who seemed pretty normal to me, but I'm sure everyone else assumes they are heavy into drugs. And maybe they are. I know Spencer uses. But I guess I couldn't say for sure about the rest of them. But even if they do, does that mean I should shun them? I don't think so.

SAME BENEATH
beneath our layers of fashion
and hair and pretension
aren't we really the same?
don't we breathe the same air?
pump red blood through our veins?
aren't we made up of bone and flesh
and DNA?
so what's the big deal?
why go and differentiate?
why not simply celebrate
that we are really the same
the same underneath
and our differences are only skin deep
cm

Four

Friday, September 20

After a somewhat uneventful week—although Tiffany got in a few verbal jabs that I'm trying to ignore—I got up the nerve to go to the Paradiso Café (the new coffeehouse in town) to inquire about performing.

First I ordered a cappuccino and sat down then proceeded to carefully evaluate the joint. There's a large coffee bar off to one side with all your typical espresso and coffee machines looking sturdy and impressive. This was surrounded by a long copper-topped counter where you can order your coffee as well as other things like pastry and bagels and juice. The floor was a checkerboard of large black and white tiles with small dark wood tables and mismatched chairs casually arranged. Two of the walls have nothing but windows, and the others have large, colorful European-type posters that look like old advertisements.

And then, here's the important part, off in a back corner is a small stage, only about a foot higher than the floor and filled with stacks of chairs and stuff. Also there are a couple of large potted plants, palms as I recall. But all in all I'd have to describe the place as pretty cool. So finally, when no one was at the counter, I got up the nerve to introduce myself.

"Hi." I forced a stiff smile. "My name is Chloe Miller; I'm a musician and this is my demo." I held up the cassette that I'd recorded last week. I wanted to get this over with as quickly and painlessly as possible and to make my escape before anyone noticed me making a complete fool of myself.

The guy behind the counter looked at me as if he thought I was about twelve years old. "You have a demo?"

"Well, it's just homemade, but I think it'll give you the general idea."

Then turning from me, he ran steam through the espresso machine to create a horrible hissing sound. "Have you ever performed?" he asked as he turned around.

"Sure." Now this wasn't a complete lie because I have played in front of people before, at least a few times anyway.

"What's your style?"

"I do a variety of stuff, but the songs on this demo are kind of like Alanis Morissette or Sheryl Crow or Aimee Mann. Kind of the old stuff."

"Old?" His brows lifted, then he nodded. "Yeah,

well, we could probably handle something like that in here." Then he leaned over the counter and peered at me. "But are you any good?"

"My choir teacher says I am."

He laughed and held out his hand for the tape. "Okay then. My name is Mike, and I run this place. I'll try to listen to your tape if I can find the time." Then he set it into a basket full of other tapes and CDs at the end of the counter.

Trying not to stare at all of those tapes, I forced another smile. "Thanks, Mike."

"But, hey, you look more like a punk rocker to me," he said as I was turning to leave.

"Yeah, well, sometimes I play like that. But you really need a backup band to produce that kind of sound in a legitimate way."

He nodded. "And this place is probably too small for all that kind of sound equipment anyway."

So, despite the basket of tapes, I feel pretty good today. At least mine is on top now. Afterward I came home and actually cleaned my room and then practiced my music for a couple hours—just in case Mike called.

On another note, I've been kind of hanging with Spencer and Allie and the others lately. It's mostly due to loneliness as well as an attempt to avoid being alone in case Tiffany and her monkeys get into the violent mode again. I usually just eat lunch and hang with them when I see them in the halls and stuff. But today, after the guys abandoned the lunch table to go outside and "get some fresh air" (I'm guessing to share a joint), Allie asked me what I was up to this weekend.

"I'm sure not going to the game tonight," I said as I sipped my soda.

"Yeah, count me out too. Besides, I heard they're supposed to lose anyway."

"It wouldn't matter to me whether they won or lost. I had to watch enough football with my two older brothers that I don't care if I never sit through another game."

"I'm not much into sports either," she said as she drummed her hands on the table.

Now I'd already noticed that Allie was always kind of hyped-up. She's constantly fidgeting or drumming her fingers on the table—as if she can't sit still. I guess I just believed that meant she was a user. But this thought made me feel bad.

"So, do you want to do something then?" Her bright blue eyes looked hopeful. "This weekend, I mean."

I studied her. "Can I be honest with you?"

She rolled her eyes. "Somehow I never like the sound of those words. Like you're going to tell me to go take a leap or that I have BO or my breath stinks." She leaned back. "Oh, fine, go ahead."

"No, it's nothing like that. But I know that Spencer uses. I mean, he told me so. And the other guys probably do too. That's not really a problem for me, but I'm not personally into that. I mean, I like you guys and everything, but I just don't want—"

"You think I use drugs?" She laughed. "Well, you already know that I smoke cigarettes, and I'll confess I've smoked pot occasionally. Who hasn't? But I'm not really looking to get hooked on something bad, you know? I mean, I don't judge Spencer and Jake. And I'm really not sure how much Cesar does drugs 'cause he told me he's trying to stay clean so he can get a job with his uncle at Home Depot, and they do regular drug testing there. But I'm not really into stuff like that. I just happen to like hanging with these guys, and besides, they're the only ones who wanted to be friends with me. So like, what am I supposed to do?"

"Yeah, that's cool. That's kinda how it is with me too. But I guess I have some hang-ups about drugs personally. I mean, my brother got pretty messed up, and I just don't really want to go there."

Allie nodded. "Me neither. So, you can just relax about that. But as I was saying, you want to do something this weekend?"

"Sure, like what?"

"Well, I'd invite you over to my place, but my mom's got something going on this weekend and—"

"Why don't you come over to my house?"

"Okay. You mean like tomorrow?"

"Sure, tomorrow's great." I knew I should probably check with my parents since they entertain a lot and might not be too thrilled if I have someone over, but then I hadn't heard of anything going on. And I figured they should be glad to see me having a friend over—especially someone who <u>wasn't</u> into drugs. And as I studied Allie, I realized they might even think she looked like a normal girl. Other than her clothes and the tiny diamond stud in her nose, in some ways she even reminded me of Caitlin, and my parents think she's the greatest.

So maybe this is the beginning of a friendship. Who knows?

Okay, I want to quit writing now, but I know I've been avoiding something in my diary. It's as if I'm trying to sweep something big under the rug. It's that whole talking to God thing. I made the mistake of e-mailing Caitlin and telling her that I'd tried it. And of course, she was so happy and is even saying that this is the "beginning of something big." And well, now I just want to forget the whole thing—cold feet, you know. I guess I'm scared that I could be entering into some-

thing I'm not really ready for. In fact, it's really
similar to the way I feel about drugs. Although
I'm sure that makes no sense. But it's true. I'm
just not ready for either of those—drugs or God.

RELIGION AND DRUGS
i'm not wanting
inhibitions
or conditions
that make me hang
by a thread
i can't handle
all the scandal
propaganda
that injects me
with such dread
i'm not ready
for addiction
or conviction
that makes me feel
like i'm dead
i may be lost
but it's my choice
and if i'm tossed
or lose my voice
i'll just remember
what I have said
cm

Sunday, September 22

I waited around all day and Allie didn't come over until after five o'clock yesterday, but then she didn't go home until around two today. I hadn't actually asked her to spend the night, but hey, that was okay. And fortunately my parents were cool, and they even sort of acted as if they liked her—in their chilly and impervious way. Why are they like that?

But I have to admit it was pretty funny when I introduced her to them because I couldn't even remember her last name. I guess I hadn't thought of it since middle school.

"This is Allie—uh—" I looked at Allie then bit my lip.

"Curtis," she said with a grin. "Allie Curtis." Then she shook my hand. "Glad to make your acquaintance—uh—Clara?"

I laughed. "Sorry."

"It's nice to meet you, Allie," my dad said, as if he was doing me a favor. "Are you new in town?"

Then she explained how they'd lived here a few years ago. "But then my dad's job got transferred, then my parents got divorced, and my mom decided to come back to her hometown."

"Oh, your mom's from here originally? Did she go to school here?" This came from my mom, always trying to make connections. It drives me nuts. "Maybe we knew her back then."

"Her maiden name was Thornton, Elise Thornton." Allie waited for them to respond.

"No." My mother shook her head. "Doesn't sound familiar."

Then Dad jumped in. "Well, I'm sure you two won't mind if we old fogies skip out on you and take in a film tonight."

"Not at all, Dad," I said, relieved to have the house to ourselves.

"There's a pizza in the freezer if you want." Mom slipped on her coat.

After they left, Allie walked around our house and just kept saying things like, "Man, I didn't know you were so rich."

"We're not rich."

She rolled her eyes. "Says you." She ran her hand over Mom's grand piano, looking at the photos lined up in their polished silver frames. "Who's this?" She stopped at a picture of Josh. "What a hottee. Can I meet him?"

"That's my brother Josh. But don't get your hopes up; he's almost twenty and he's into religion."

"Religion?" She frowned. "You mean like studying for the priesthood? Because I think that's a sin—not allowing priests and nuns to get married."

I laughed. "No, he's not going to become a priest."

"Okay then. How can I meet this hunk?"

I took the photo from her hands and set it back on the piano. "Forget about him, Allie. He's in love with someone else."

"That's not fair." She made a face. "I <u>hate</u> her."

I smiled. "Actually she's a really nice girl."

Allie shook her head. "I doubt it. Besides, I <u>hate</u> really nice girls. They give me the creeps." Then she folded her arms across her chest. "I guess I'll just cast a spell on her."

I watched her as she closed her eyes and took on a very serious expression. "Are you losing it? Or maybe you watched one too many episodes of <u>Sabrina, the Teenage Witch?</u>"

She opened her eyes and laughed. "No! And I wouldn't really put a spell on your brother's girlfriend. That would be wrong."

"What're you talking about?"

"Haven't you ever heard of Wicca?"

"Yeah, a little. Are you into that?" I studied her closely. "I mean, are you really a witch?"

"I don't ride a broomstick or wear a pointy hat or anything, but I am learning about witchcraft."

"Really?"

"Yeah, I've ordered a couple things from this really cool website. It's fun and makes a lot of sense to me."

"Like how?"

"Well, the craft isn't about casting mean

spells. You're not even supposed to hurt people. The motto is something like: If it doesn't hurt anyone then it's okay. That's not exactly right, but it's something like that."

"So what is it about then?"

"I guess it's kind of a religion, but they don't call it a religion."

"So do they worship the devil and stuff like you see in movies?"

"They don't believe in the devil."

"Do they believe in God?"

"Not exactly. It's more like the god in you—like there's a goddess inside you, and you have the magical powers to control your life, for good of course."

"And just how do you do that exactly?"

"I'm not totally sure about all the details yet. You have to read and memorize a lot of stuff. And then you make these things, kind of like witch tools to help you—but you're the only one who can make them or they don't work right. Then you study these spells and charts and stuff and learn about herbs and read their books. You can even take their seminars, but it's pretty expensive."

"Sounds pretty complicated too."

She frowned. "Yeah, it is, a little."

"But you think it's legit—like it's really true?"

She nodded. "It sounds pretty good to me."

"But is it true? Or are they just pulling your leg and getting you to buy a bunch of worthless crud."

"No, it's for real, Chloe. Witchcraft has been around since the beginning of time. Way longer than any other religion."

I thought about that. "But does that mean it's right?"

"Well, I'm sure your gorgeous brother would think it's wrong." She grew thoughtful. "Unless I put a spell on him to convince him otherwise."

"You would do that?"

"No, not really. That would probably be wrong. But I do think witchcraft is right. Because it's right for me. I need some answers for my life. I want to feel like I have some control, you know? Not as if I'm getting tossed about like a leaf in the wind."

"Yeah, I know what you mean."

We talked about Wicca some more, but the more she told me about it, the more confusing it became. And I could tell that she still didn't fully understand it herself. "I guess it's fine for you, if you really believe in it. I just wish it made more sense," I finally said.

"Well, I'll keep reading and studying, then I'll try to explain it better."

We went up to my room and she immediately spotted my guitar. "Do you play that?"

"Sure." I picked it up and strummed a few chords.

"But do you know any songs?"

"Yeah, a few. But I mostly just play my own songs."

"Your own songs?"

"Yeah. I make them up."

"Cool. Wanna play one for me?"

So I played one of my earlier songs called "Cinderella Shortcut." It's about a girl who was always kicked around by her older sisters until she locked them both in the hall closet then ran off to the dance without them.

Allie laughed. "That's hilarious. You really wrote that?"

I nodded. Then I told her about my demo tape and the coffeehouse.

"You could be performing at the Paradiso! That's like almost famous!"

"The key word being almost."

"I wish I were a musician," she said. "I mean, I like to sing and everything, but I don't play an instrument." But even as she said this she was drumming her fingers on top of my guitar.

"How about being a drummer?" I suggested suddenly, pointing down at her fidgeting hands. We both laughed.

"Yeah, my mom's always on my case because I'm always thumping on something. Just tell me if I get on your nerves. I forget that I'm doing it. I was diagnosed as hyperactive in second grade, and they had me on Ritalin for years. Maybe that's why I'm not into drugs now. I quit taking the Ritalin last summer. And I'm probably more hyper than ever now, but I feel more alive too."

"Seriously, Allie, how about taking up the drums?"

"Oh, yeah, sure. I'd love to. Sounds great." She folded her hands tightly together and placed them in her lap as if she were trying to keep them still. "But, hey, I might as well come clean since you'll figure it all out sooner or later anyway."

I watched her as she looked down at her hands, a grim expression on her face. "What are you talking about, Allie?"

"Well..." She looked up at me. "After seeing all this... I mean, like your parents and your big fancy house... I guess you might as well know that... okay, let's just say I won't be inviting you over to my place anytime soon."

I knew what she meant. But I just waved my hand as if I could wave it all away. "Oh, that. Sheesh, you shouldn't worry about that. I mean, I'm not at all like my parents when it comes to money. I'm not into this material stuff at all."

"That just seems totally unfair."

"Huh?"

She laughed now. "Because, hey, I'd switch

places with you in a heartbeat. I could seriously get into all this material stuff real easy. It's only the people who have money who act as if it's not important. The rest of us know what it's like without it."

"Well, maybe you should do one of your Wicca spells and see if you can make yourself rich. Or maybe you could switch us around. I really don't think I'd mind being poor. I mean, look at how I dress."

She made a face. "So, anyway, that's why it's easy for you to say, 'Sure, why not take up the drums, Allie?' Do you have any idea what a drum set would cost? And then, how the crud would I pay for lessons?"

Suddenly I remembered something. "Hey, I think we still have an old drum set."

"You're kidding."

"No, seriously. My brother was into drums for a while."

"You mean Josh." She got that dreamy look again.

"Yeah, he was playing with some friends who were trying to start this band. But I don't think he ever actually practiced, and they eventually kicked him out."

"Cool. I wouldn't mind playing on Josh's drums."

I rolled my eyes. "Well, if you think they'll be

all full of good vibes, you better—" But before I could finish she cut me off with the chorus of that corny old Beach Boys song.

She grabbed my hairbrush, holding it like a microphone, and started belting out goofy lyrics about good vibrations in a husky alto voice that was actually pretty good.

Pretty soon, I had to join in and we had ourselves a pretty good little duet, although she definitely knew the lyrics way better than me.

"Do you honestly like the Beach Boys?" I asked when we'd finally worn it out.

She laughed. "No, but my mom definitely does." Then she made a face. "But I'm warning you: Don't go laughing at me for liking the Dixie Chicks, or I'll have to leave right now."

I grinned. "Actually, I kind of like them too. Although I don't usually admit it to anyone."

"So what about those drums?"

"I think they're still up in the attic. I used to go up there and just wail on them when I was little, and I don't think anyone's ever moved them."

"But still I couldn't afford to—"

"Oh, don't worry. You could probably just have them. Or maybe borrow them. Or wait!" I stood up and started pacing across my room.

"What? You're creepin' me out, Chloe. You look like some mad scientist who's going to sew body parts together to—"

"That's it! We could set them up in the pool-room."

"Poolroom? You guys have a poolroom? Do you have an indoor swimming pool too?"

"Yeah, you bet. And a bowling alley and a tennis court and a movie theater—"

"Oh, come on."

"No, silly, it's just an old pool table that's set up in an unfinished space above the garage. Josh and his friends used to hang out there when he was in high school."

"Hey, I wouldn't complain about a pool table at my place—well, except for the fact it wouldn't fit. So, what are we waiting for? And after we move those drums we can shoot us some snookers. Bet I can beat you too."

And so we spent the evening knocking around and moving the drum set and fixing pizza and playing pool. It was actually pretty fun. And I almost told my mom that I was happy today, but that might've been going overboard.

But I'm still not completely sure about Allie. I mean, I really like her. But there's just something that makes me uncomfortable. I don't know if it's all her witch talk or her hyperness. Or maybe it's just me. But she's fun and I do like her. Not only that, but she might have the makings of a musician in her. And after I showed her the correct way to hold the drumsticks (I remembered from when Josh taught me), she seemed to take right to drumming.

I've no doubt she'll need some real lessons, but we played some CDs and tried to play along, and it was pretty hilarious. Still, I'm not sure that Allie has what it takes to be a really close friend. And that makes me kind of sad. Like maybe I'm too picky.

I got an e-mail from Caitlin today. She seems lonely, and I've been trying to encourage her not to give up on her roommate (who actually sounds like someone I would be friends with, although she's a little on the mean side). But last week, I'd told Caitlin how I was struggling to understand what's real truth and what's not. And now, after hearing Allie go on about Wicca, I feel even more confused.

But in Caitlin's e-mail, she challenged me to find a Bible that has Jesus' words written in red— so they show up in contrast against the black words. "And then try to read only the redlines," she said. "I know you're not into the Bible. But give it a try. Just the redlines." So today, after Allie went home, I rode the bus over to the mall and went into the Christian bookstore where the lady looked at me like I had accidentally walked into the wrong place. But then I said, "Do you have those Bibles where Jesus' words are written in red?"

She smiled. "Sure, honey, they're right over here."

And so tonight, I was just reading the red-lines. But I only read three pieces—the first ones I found. And the weird thing is that these three verses almost make sense to me. Almost. And for the first time in several days I actually tried talking to God again. I asked him to show me what's the truth and what's not and to show me whether he's for real or not. I figure it can't hurt to ask.

JUST THE REDLINES
jesus says:
bread alone won't keep you alive
you need the word of god to survive
he says:
do not tempt the lord your god
and he says:
be gone, satan!
only worship and serve god

Five

Sunday, September 29

I called Josh over and over last week, and after leaving about three messages he finally called back. "What's up, sis?"

"Sheesh, I can't believe it's really you. I thought you might've moved to another country or something. Don't you ever stay home?"

He laughed. "There's a lot going on here. But let's not talk about that. How are you? How's high school?"

Without going into all the grueling details, I managed to paint a fairly positive picture. Then I asked, "Remember your old drum set?"

"Sure. Are you planning on taking up drums now too? Going to become a one-woman band?"

"No. But I have a friend and she's kinda poor, you know, and she wants to play drums."

"Give them to her. I'm sure Mom'll be glad to have them out of the attic."

"Thanks, Josh. She'll really appreciate it."

"Does she know how to play?"

"No, not really. But she seems like she'd be a natural. And I thought it would be fun to have someone to jam with."

"Hey, I know a guy who'd probably give her lessons for free."

"You're kidding. Who?"

"Willy Johnson. He plays drums at the church."

"At the church?" I sighed. "You mean with the hymns and stuff?"

Josh laughed. "They don't exactly do hymns at that church. Besides, Willy used to play with a pretty good rock band that toured the country in the seventies. I can't remember their name, but they actually cut a record."

"Really? And he plays at the church? The one you and Caitlin went to?"

"Yeah. Call up Pastor Tony and he'll give you Willy's number."

We talked a little longer, then he told me Tony's number. I almost told Josh that Allie was looking into becoming a witch (or possibly already was one), but I knew how he'd react. I'd probably get a long lecture or sermon, and he'd be all worried and might even change his mind about the drums. Plus he'd probably tell Caitlin. And, well, I just don't need that kind of stress right now. So I kept this information to myself.

I tried to call Allie last night but kept getting the busy signal. At first I was irritated, thinking why doesn't she have call-waiting or e-mail, then I remembered that costs more money—so much I take for granted! I also remembered how she said her mom talks on the phone a lot. So I decided not to hold it against Allie.

The next morning, I spotted Allie in the hallway and immediately told her the good news.

"You're kidding? Free drums and lessons?" Her eyes lit up. "I think this Wicca thing is really working for me. It's like good karma."

That's probably when I made a strange face.

"What's wrong?"

"Well, the guy who might be willing to give the free lessons plays drums in a church."

"In a church? I didn't know they allowed drums in churches."

"Apparently they do in this one."

She shrugged. "Well, is he a good drummer?"

"Josh says so. He played in a rock band that actually cut a record in the seventies."

"That's cool. If he doesn't mind teaching someone like me, I don't mind learning from someone like him." She paused. "Well, as long as he doesn't try to convert me, that is."

So later that afternoon, I called up Tony Berringer and told him I was Josh's sister and that he'd recommended Willy as someone who could teach drums.

"I remember you," he said. "You helped Caitlin out with the cultural fair last year."

"Yeah, that's right." I'd almost forgotten about that.

"Are you going to be involved again this year?"

"I don't know. Maybe."

"Great." Then he gave me Willy's number.

"Uh, Mr. Berringer?"

"Just call me Tony. Everyone else does."

"Okay. But can I ask you a question? And can I trust you with some sort of client privilege or whatever you might call it in your profession?"

"Of course, Chloe. It comes with my job. What's up?"

"Well, it's about my friend, the one who needs free drumming lessons. The thing is, she's into witchcraft or Wicca. And I just don't want this whole thing to turn into something ugly, you know? Like if Willy found out she's a witch and then got mad. Or if he tried to convert her and made her feel bad. Do you understand what I'm saying?"

"Yes. And I don't think you need to worry. Willy is a good guy. And he's seen a lot of stuff. I don't think he'd judge your friend for her beliefs."

"But would he try to convert her?"

"I don't think so. But I'm sure he'll be honest about what he believes."

"That's okay. I mean, that seems pretty normal to me."

So after I hung up, I decided to call this Willy guy myself. I thought it might be better to just lay the cards on the table, in case he wasn't interested in giving lessons to a witch, or even a wannabe witch.

But Willy was cool. When I told him what Allie was into, he acted as if it was no big deal. "Hey, I used to dabble in those same kinds of things myself," he told me. "Man, I was into all sorts of weird stuff during the seventies."

"So you won't try to convert her?" I asked just to be sure.

He laughed. "It's my belief that only God can do the converting. I try to love and respect people for who they are. I leave the rest of the business to God."

"Sounds good to me."

So it's all set. Allie's first lesson is on Tuesday at five. Fortunately her apartment complex is only a few blocks from the church—that's where Willy's going to teach her, since he keeps his drum set there. He said he'll see how it goes before he decides whether it'll be a regular thing or not. "I don't mean to sound exclusive," he told me, "but I don't like to waste my time on someone with no talent."

"Hey, that sounds fair to me. She's never had a

lesson but she's been playing around on my brother's old drum set, and I think she has talent."

"Well, we'll see."

WITCH ON DRUMS
okay, witchy woman
go 'head and cast your spell
let's see if you've got rhythm
or play drums real well
old willy knows his business
and the cross is on the wall
let's see you work your magic
if it is real at all
cm

Tuesday, October 1

Allie just called. She had her first lesson with Willy and was really excited. "He says I have real talent," she gushed. "And that we can have lessons twice a week on Tuesdays and Thursdays."

"Cool. I thought you were a natural."

"But he wants me to practice every day."

"Do you want to move the drums to your place?"

"No way. My mom already said to forget it. She says we'll get kicked out of the apartment for sure if I make that kind of noise. Willy gave me a practice pad and some drumsticks to use at home. But he said I need to play on real drums at least every other day."

"That's okay. You can come over here."

"Will your parents mind?"

"If you came over right after school, they wouldn't even be home."

"Cool." She paused. "But how about you? Would you mind?"

"No, of course not. Why do you ask that?"

"Oh, I don't know. Sometimes it seems as if you're my friend, and other times I feel kinda like you're pushing me away, like maybe I irritate you. Kinda like with my mom. She says I get on her nerves. It might be that way with you."

"It's not like that at all." But even as I said the words I knew it wasn't totally true. "But I'm at a weird place right now. It's like I'm trying to figure things out about myself and a lot of things, and maybe I'm just sort of confused. You know?"

"Yeah. That's how I felt before I found out about Wicca. But it's like helping me to feel more centered."

I didn't mention how she seemed a little off center to me sometimes, because, hey, who knows? Maybe that's centered for her. But I think I want something more for my life. I'm just not sure what it is.

Tonight I read the redlines again. So far I've read some things I kind of get. Like the section that talks about when people are poor or meek or hungry and how things will improve for them eventually. It made me think that Jesus really cared about the down-and-outers. I like that. But I've also read some things that confuse me. Like how we're not supposed to be angry and that being angry is as bad as murdering someone.

Now I just don't get that. I mean, I'm still angry with Tiffany and her thugs. But, hey, I didn't murder them. Okay, I wanted to back then, but I don't really want to now. Just the same, I'm still angry and I don't think I'll ever forgive them—especially that Tiffany dweeb. And if looks could kill, I swear that girl would be dead a hundred times over. But then so would I. So what's up with this anger thing? Does Jesus honestly expect me not to be angry? Those girls beat me up for absolutely no reason, except that I look different. Why shouldn't I be angry?

SOMETHING'S MISSING
my life's a puzzle
pieces strewn
in a tantrum
'cross my room
missing words
that never rhyme

thoughts that tumble
through my mind
socks get lost
in the dryer
where do i
go find the fire
passion burns
a cigarette
that goes out
when it gets wet
what is real
the missing part
that will heal
this aching heart?
cm

Friday, October 4

Allie wasn't too pleased to hear that I'd invited
Laura Mitchell over to jam with us tomorrow.

"Why her?" she asked when I told her at lunch
today.

I set down my fork. "Why not?"

"Laura Mitchell? She seems pretty cool."
Spencer peered over at Allie. "What's up with you
anyway? You got some kind of bigotry going on or
something?"

Allie tossed a blistering look his way.

"Yeah, Allie." Cesar pointed his finger at her.

"You got something against folks who ain't as white as you?"

"You guys make me sick!" She stood up as if she were going to leave.

"Hey, chill, Allie," I said quietly. "They're just teasing."

She sat back down.

"But what's the deal, Al?" Spencer continued. "You got a problem with Laura?"

"That's not it."

"Well, what is it then?" I looked her right in the eye. "Because if you've got a problem with Laura, I want to know what it is."

She shrugged. "It's not a racial thing. I just don't think she'd want to do the same kind of music that we want to do."

"What kind of music do you think she'd want to do?" asked Cesar. "Rap?" He started rapping out a beat on the table. "You think that cuz that girl is black, all she know to do is rap? Just cuz she ain't white as you, ya think she can't do music too?"

We all laughed and Allie looked slightly mortified. "I don't know," she said quietly.

"Okay, guys, no more teasing," I said. "Allie, that's not it, is it? You're not judging her just because she's different."

"I really don't want to talk about this anymore." Allie stared down at her lunch.

"Maybe you need to talk about it," I said. "And you're with friends."

Cesar reached over and patted her arm. "Hey, I'm just fooling with ya. We all have our hang-ups, Al." He pointed at Jake. "Man, Jake just about threw me off the balcony yesterday when I called him Carrottop. And I get pretty fried when Spencer calls me Taco Bell. Man, I don't even eat tacos."

Allie looked up. "I shouldn't have said that about Laura. I'm sorry. The truth is I've never had a—an African-American friend."

I smiled. "Well, maybe it's time. And if it makes you feel any better, Laura has an amazing voice and she's great at harmony—a perfect second soprano."

"But I thought you were a second soprano," said Allie.

"That's what I sing in choir, but I've got a wide range."

"So what's up anyway?" asked Jake. "Are you guys putting together a chick band?"

"Like the Spice Girls?" teased Cesar.

"Ugh!" I punched him in the arm.

"Or maybe you're going to all dye your hair blond and be the Dixie Chicks," said Jake.

"One of them isn't blond anymore," said Allie.

"We're just getting together to jam and have fun," I finally said. "Let's just leave it at that."

"But did you know that Chloe might be playing at the Paradiso Cafe?"

"Allie!" I scowled at her.

"Well, it's true!"

"Really?" Cesar looked at me with interest. "That's a cool place. I heard they're going to start having live music sometime this fall."

"Yeah, and Chloe might be up there before long."

"I've never even heard back from the manager. He probably hated my demo."

"You have a demo?" Cesar looked really impressed now.

"You know what a demo is?"

"I'm not stupid." Cesar set down his cup. "I happen to know a little bit about music. I've got an uncle who works at a sound studio and—"

"Man, how many uncles do you have?" asked Jake.

"Hey, you know how those hot-blooded Latino men are," said Cesar putting on a thick Hispanic accent. "They like having big families."

Spencer rolled his eyes. "I've gotta get outta here and get some fresh air. You guys coming?"

Jake got up but Cesar remained. "No, I'm going to stay here and talk music with the Spice Girls."

"Oh, puleeze," cried Allie. "You're gonna make me hurl."

"Hey, you're the one who ate that junk they

call pizza," he said. "It'll be your own fault if you get sick."

"So are you going to be okay with it, Allie?" I asked.

"With what? The pizza?"

"No. I mean with Laura coming to jam. Are you okay?"

She slowly nodded. "I suppose you guys were kinda right. I may have some hang-ups about blacks. The truth is my dad grew up in a really racist family, and he's got some serious bigotry going on in his head. And as much as I always say I disagree with him about that stuff, well, I'm afraid some of his garbage may have rubbed off on me too." She sighed. "I think it'll be good for me to get to know Laura. I need to get past this."

I smiled. "That's cool, Allie. I'm glad you could be honest about this."

"Yeah, and you're really not alone," said Cesar. "I think everyone has some sort of prejudice going on. Take our little Chloe here. She thinks she has it all together, but I know she's got her problems."

"What do you mean? I'm not prejudiced. I like everyone for who they are."

"Okay then." He nodded to a table on the other side of the cafeteria. "How about those preppy chicks over there. How do you feel about them?"

I shrugged. "Hey, it's their life. If they want to live it by being shallow and superficial, well, that's their choice."

"So you think they are all shallow and superficial," said Cesar. "That sounds like prejudice to me."

I thought about that. "Okay, maybe you're right. I don't personally know everyone at that table, so I shouldn't categorize them all together."

"Hey, don't feel bad. I do the same thing myself." He leaned back in his chair. "But maybe it's time to start thinking differently."

"But that's what they want," countered Allie. "They _like_ being alike. Can't you tell by the way they dress and act and talk? They thrive on their sameness. "

Cesar nodded. "Good point. But still you could be wrong."

"What makes you such an expert?" I asked him.

"Being on the other end," he said soberly.

"Okay, that makes sense. But you're not the only one. Allie and I both know what it feels like to be judged by our appearances."

"Yes—" he held up a finger—"but you both have control over that. You don't _have_ to dress the way you do. I, on the other hand, can dress just like the jocks or the preppy boys, but I am still judged by my skin color."

"I like your skin color." I think I must've blushed as soon as the words escaped my mouth.

Cesar smiled. "Hey, I like yours too."

"How about mine?" asked Allie to my relief. Then she pulled up her sweater sleeve to reveal a pale arm. "Sheesh, my tan is almost completely gone now."

"Yeah, yours is cool too." Cesar patted her arm then started singing the old Paul McCartney song, "Ebony and Ivory." We joined him as best we could until the bell rang and reminded us it was almost time for fifth period.

But after that conversation I have a lot more respect for Cesar. He usually acts so goofy that you can never take him seriously. But now I'm seeing him in a different light. Not only is he easy to look at, but I think I really like him.

FALLING
tumbling, bumbling, stumbling down
falling, sprawling on the ground
elusive and intrusive things
fragile as butterfly wings
daisy petals one by one
scattered in the summer sun
does he love me, love me not
is he burning, is he hot
can i, am i willing, able

lay my card upon the table
will it be the queen of hearts
the place where all the hurting starts
cm

Six

Sunday, October 6

I gave myself a long, stern lecture and a cold shower and have determined to keep Cesar out of my head and my heart. I do not want to, cannot afford to, fall in love right now. How do I know this? Because I have given my heart away before and was deeply hurt—so hurt I could barely function. Oh, sure, people say you can't fall in love when you're only fourteen. But what do they know of my heart or me? And its complexities. Even I don't attempt to explain such things. Slippery and invisible things that the mind can't understand. All I know is that I must stay on track here. I must continue this search for—myself—truth—and whatever it is that I must eventually find or die trying. And I must stay focused on my music.

So, now I know; Cesar must remain only a good friend. And I don't think you can have too many good friends. That is, if they're truly good friends. How do I define a good friend? Someone who is there for you, believes in you, is loyal to you, is honest with you, and wants what's best for you—is that too much to ask? Okay, I realize those are some pretty big shoes to fill. But I think, hey, if you don't set your expectations high enough, you might end up settling for less than the best that life has to offer you. I'm not settling.

Since I have decided to make music my main focus, I'm pleased to report that Allie, Laura, and I had our first official jam session. There was only one problem: With Laura's bass with its amp system and Allie blasting away on drums (and she may be better, but she still needs work), my guitar (only an acoustic) was completely blown away. And though I don't ever plan to completely give up my acoustic guitar altogether, I do plan to wage an all-out campaign for a good electric guitar and decent amplifier.

I've already started checking the classifieds and am willing to pay for half with my savings, but I think my parents should pitch in too. After all, they can certainly afford it. So, right now, I am keeping my room clean and trying to act (not look) like a normal girl. While my mother seems pleased, my father looks slightly suspicious. But later this week, after I've located the perfect guitar, I'll break the news.

Allie came over to practice on the drums again tonight (my parents went to dinner with friends), and I asked her what she thought about Laura. We hadn't had a chance to have this conversation yesterday.

"She's nice."

"Nice?" Now that's not the kind of word that Allie normally uses as a compliment.

"Okay, maybe nice was too strong. But she seems kind of, oh, I don't know and honestly this has nothing to with prejudice. But she seems, well, too good, you know what I mean?"

"Too good?" I thought about that. "You mean because she talked about singing in her church?"

Allie pointed her finger at me. "Bingo! Stuff like that. It weirds me out a little and kinda makes me nervous."

"But you're taking drumming lessons in a church," I reminded her. "Does that weird you out too?"

She laughed. "Nah, Willy's cool. And I think, hey, if they're willing to let a witch in their church, how bad can they really be?"

"So you really do think of yourself as a witch then?"

"Well, not officially. But I have a feeling if I told regular church people, like Laura for instance, what I really believe, they'd probably call me a witch for sure. And if it was a few hundred years ago, they'd be having a big weenie roast and using me for the kindling."

I laughed. "Pretty picture, Allie. But back to

Laura. Do you like her?"

She shrugged. "I don't dislike her, if that's what you mean. She just makes me uncomfortable."

"Do you think you might make her uncomfortable?"

"Hey, I only mentioned Wicca once, and when I saw her expression, I shut right up about it."

I patted her on the back. "Oh, good girl."

"Well, I just don't think she likes me very much."

"What makes you think that?"

"For one thing, she never once looked right at me. And whenever she has a question or anything, she always directs it to you."

"But I'm kind of the leader of this group."

Allie nodded. "That's another thing that bugs me. If we do decide to have a group, are you automatically the leader?"

Well, I wasn't sure what to say to that. I was thinking: Of course, I'm the leader, you nitwit! This is my house, my music, my drum set, my idea.... "Who do you think should be the leader?" I asked calmly.

She seemed to consider this, then finally said, "I guess it should be you."

"Do you want to have a vote?"

She grinned. "Nah, I don't think that's necessary."

"Good. Besides, we're only jamming; we're not forming a band. We're not even close to ready for something like that."

"Why?"

I looked at her little chin sticking out like she was offended, and in spite of myself I cracked up. "For starters, Ringo, you can barely play drums."

"Hey, Willy says I get better every day."

"Yeah, after what—two lessons?"

"Well, I'm a fast learner."

I gave her my best don't-give-up-hope smile. "Yes, you're doing really great, Al. But the thing is, I'm not ready to really form a band yet. And if we do decide to take it to the next level, I want to do it right. I mean, sheesh—I don't even have the right kind of guitar."

She looked down at my acoustic. "Yeah, we pretty much blasted you outta the waters didn't we?"

"Pretty much. But I'm already working on getting something else."

"I figured." She set down her drumsticks. "Looks like I've done enough damage here. Wanna lose a game of pool to me now?"

And so I did. Then after the game she went home. I went downstairs and actually straightened up the house. I loaded the dishwasher and even put in soap and turned it on! That ought to impress the parents. Then I went to my room and cleaned it, well, sort of. Then I did my homework, and even read my redlines. But tonight I came across some stuff that is just too much. I'm thinking maybe I've had enough of these redlines because I simply cannot accept this.

Jesus says (and I'll admit I've heard this before, who hasn't?) that we need to love our neighbor. Okay, that's simple enough. But then he says we need to love our enemies too. Not only that, but if they slap you on your right cheek you're supposed to turn around and offer them your left cheek too. Well, when Tiffany slapped me (and then Kerry followed her lead), I never in a thousand years would've been able to say, "Hey, why not have a go at my other cheek while you're beating me up?" I mean, how crazy is that?

And then Jesus goes on to say that if someone demands your overcoat that you should give him your jacket as well. But I'm thinking, hang on a minute. If someone takes one coat from you, what the pickle do they need another one for? It just doesn't make sense.

And then to top it all off, Jesus says that we're supposed to give to anyone who asks us for something. Now I'm not totally opposed to that, because I like giving to people who really need it—like the homeless or the kids down in Mexico

that Josh and Caitlin help out. But what if someone who isn't even poor asked me to hand over
some money? Or worse yet, what if someone like
Tiffany asked me?

So, I'm sorry, but this does not, I repeat DOES
NOT, compute. I just do NOT get it. Why does Jesus
talk in such riddles anyway? And how is it that
anyone takes him seriously? Or do people just
dismiss the things that he taught if they don't
understand it? And if that's the case, then what
kind of religion is this? Right now it doesn't
make any more sense to me than Allie's convo-
luted Wicca rules. I don't get it!

SHOW ME
all is murky, thick, and dark
i cannot see or hear or feel
a wall surrounds me cold and stark
a barrier for what is real
i am blind and deaf and dumb
wrapped and trapped inside this tomb
to this death i will succumb
the air i breathe is full of doom
where is life and truth and light?
why is it so hard to see?
show me how to know what's right
show me what's inside of me
cm

Wednesday, October 9

I'm not sure what's wrong with me today. But all morning long I felt like crying. I barely made it through my classes, then right after choir, I streaked out the door before anyone could witness the tears coming down my face. But somehow Laura knew something was wrong, and she actually trailed me clear down past our locker bay and into the bathroom. I was standing in a stall blowing my nose and trying to control myself when I heard her voice.

"Is that you, Chloe?"

"Huh?"

"Up here."

I looked up to see her big brown eyes staring at me from the next stall. "Wh—what?"

"Sorry, but you seemed upset."

I blew my nose again then shook my head as if I might be able to shake it all off. "Yeah, it's weird. There's nothing seriously wrong or anything, but I feel really awful. I don't know what's wrong with me today."

"You wanna talk?"

"I guess. Although I'm not sure what good it'll do."

So we grabbed some lunch, took it out to the patio, and sat down. Fortunately, the sun was out, and other than a chilly breeze it wasn't too bad out there. "So, what's up?" she asked as I sipped on my soda.

"I honestly don't know. I just feel really, really sad."

She nodded and picked up a french fry. "Maybe it's my fault."

I set down my drink. "Your fault? Are you kidding?"

"No. I might have something to do with this."

"Huh? I don't get it." About then I was wondering if maybe Laura was secretly into Wicca too, as though maybe she thought she'd cast some sort of evil spell on me.

"The thing is, I've been praying for you, Chloe."

I looked at her then kinda laughed. "Well, hey, join the club. My brother and his girlfriend have both been praying for me too—for more than a year now. And who knows who else has me on their God hit list."

"Really? How do you know they're praying?"

"It's not like they keep it a secret."

She smiled. "Do you mind? I mean, that we're all praying for you?"

I shook my head. "But I guess I wonder, why all the fuss?"

She picked up another fry and dipped it in ketchup, turning it slowly in a circle. "I guess I'm praying because it seemed to me that you're kind of stuck in the middle."

"In the middle?"

"Yeah. I mean, you have Allie and her Wicca stuff going on, but I don't think you're really into that. And then I'm a Christian—I didn't know about your brother and stuff, but that explains it even more. And I guess I just got the feeling you were kinda strung out between two different worlds."

"You know, I do feel sorta torn apart. But I'm not sure that's why."

"I think it is. And anyway, God just put you on my heart, and I've been praying for you. For a couple of weeks now."

"Really?" The idea that a girl who barely knew me was actually praying for me was kind of intriguing. "Why would you do that?"

"Like I said, God put you on my heart."

"Well, that's nice. But I'm not real sure what that actually means." I studied her as she sipped her milk shake. "Do you?"

She looked up, the whites showing beneath her dark irises. "You really want to know what I think?"

Now I swear, as weird as this sounds, I actually had a shiver run up my spine just then. And it wasn't the air temperature because it was in the sixties and I had on a sweatshirt. I just nodded.

"Well, I think there's a battle going on for you."

I felt my eyes grow wide. "A battle?"

She nodded. "For your soul."

I swallowed.

"I think the powers of goodness and light are going up against the powers of evil and darkness right now—fighting over who's going to claim your heart."

"You're serious?"

She sighed. "I was afraid you wouldn't believe me."

"Noooo, I'm not saying I don't believe you. It just sounds so strange—so sort of ooga-booga—Twilight Zoneish, you know?"

"Yeah. I know." She looked down at her fries. "It's why I don't usually talk about this stuff."

"But you <u>really</u> believe it?"

"I <u>know</u> it."

"But why? Why would the powers of—whatever that was you said—give a flying fig about my soul?"

"Because God loves you, Chloe. He has big things for your life. And the devil wants to ruin everything." She looked me right in the eyes now. "Honestly, I've never had such a strong feeling as this before, and I swear, I've never said anything like this to anyone before. But I truly believe that God is going to do something powerful with your life—if you give him your heart, that is."

Again with the goose bumps. And then I started to cry, not big-time sobbing, but just little streams of tears flowing down my face. "But I don't get it. I've been reading the redlines and I—"

"The what?"

"The redlines. You know, the words in the Bible that Jesus said. When I read things like love your enemies—I just don't get it. I can't do it."

Now she started snickering, as if I'd said something really funny. "Well, of course not."

"Of course not?"

"No, you goofball. You're not supposed to be able to do it."

"But what's the sense in that? Why does he tell us to do it if we're not—"

"He knows we can't do it, silly. It's impossible."

"But if it's impossible, then what the—"

"It's impossible when we try to do it on our own—without Jesus. It's only when we invite Jesus into our hearts that we become able to do these things, and only with his help. And even then we still mess up sometimes. Like remember that day in the bathroom with Tiffany Knight?"

"Of course."

"I wanted to tear that creep's hair right outta her thick-headed little skull."

I smiled. "Yeah, me too. In fact, I still do."

"Well, there's the difference. I don't—not any-more."

"You don't?"

"No. Not really. But if you get me going, I'll have to go back to Jesus and ask him to help me to do better, because there's a little something in me that still wants to hate her sometimes."

"So, you honestly don't hate her?"

She shook her head. "In fact, I'm praying for her too. And I realize that she's just seriously miserable and wants everyone else to be miser-able too."

Well, now that really got my head to spinning. A lot of what Laura said actually seemed to make sense, and it had to do with some of the specific questions I've had lately. But at the same time I felt confused.

"I guess I still don't really understand that part about battling for my soul, Laura. It seems sort of overblown and unbelievable."

She seemed to consider this and finally said, "Tell me, do you believe there's evil in this world?"

I considered her question before I answered. "Yeah. I guess I do. I mean, when I think of wars that kill innocent children, or starvation that's caused by corrupt governments, or Third World countries that allow their children to be enslaved to perform hard labor, or even the bombing of the World Trade Center. Yeah, I think that's all pretty evil."

"And do you think God makes those things happen?"

I thought about that. "If he does, then I don't think I like him very much."

"Okay, let me put it another way. Do you think there's good in this world?"

I considered this. "Well, yes, but to be honest I've been focusing on the evil more than the good lately. But let me think... The beauty of nature is good—mountains and trees and oceans and sunsets. And there's goodness in little children. And when I see someone helping out their fellow man, that seems pretty good."

"Do you believe God has anything to do with those good things?"

Slowly but surely it felt as if a little light was just beginning to go on. "Yes, I think maybe he does."

"So, okay then, you do believe in good and evil?"

"Maybe I do."

"Now do you think there's power in both good and evil?"

I thought about that and finally nodded.

"Okay, you seem like a smart person to me, Chloe. If you believe in two completely opposite powers, such as good and evil, do you believe they might also experience some conflict occasionally?"

"It seems possible."

"And now, what if the two powers were after the exact same thing, do you think there might be a battle going on?"

"Man, Laura. Have you ever thought about becoming a preacher?"

She laughed. "But really, do you see what I mean?"

"I think I'm starting to. It actually makes sense to me."

"All right then. So, can you accept that it's possible that God told me to pray for you because there's a battle going on for your soul?"

"Maybe so." I studied her. "But be honest with me, does this have a lot to do with Allie and her Wicca thing? Because I'm really not into that."

"I don't think that's the main reason I felt concerned. But if it makes you feel any better, I'm praying for Allie too. And no, I don't like that she's experimenting with witchcraft, but I don't dislike her because of it. In fact, I think she's pretty cool."

"Really?"

"Yeah. I just wish she'd find the _real_ truth."

"And that is?"

"God, of course. And the fact that he sent his

son Jesus to forgive us and give us real life.
That's all you really need to know."

"It's that simple?"

She nodded. "God knew we humans didn't need
great, complex schemes to get into heaven. I
think he just wanted to keep it simple."

"So we could wrap our minds around it?"

"More like our hearts. He says all we need to
do is invite Jesus into our hearts, and then he'll
show us what to do next."

"Has it really been that simple for you?" I
watched her closely, searching for any sign of
insincerity.

"As long as I keep it that way. Sometimes I com-
plicate things with my own problems and selfish
choices. But if I hang tight with him and try to
do what he's showing me, life stays pretty simple
and good."

I frowned. "It sounds almost too good to be
true. And you know what they say about that."

"Well, you'll never know how good it is until you
believe that it's true. It's really all about faith."

We talked some more, and then it was time to go
to class. I was really thankful when the bell
rang too. I'm sure I was freaking out by then,
worried that Laura was about to ask me to pray
with her. I could just imagine us both kneeling
like nuns on the patio as kids headed to fifth
period. Yeah, sure! Anyway, I was relieved to get

away from her. All this talk was making me uncomfortable.

Still, for the rest of the afternoon, I kept thinking about what she'd said. Part of me was starting to believe it could be true, but the rest of me was cynical and skeptical. Then on my way home from school, I remembered what she'd said about the battle. Could that really be what was going on inside of me? I thought about how I feel when I have the flu, and there's a battle going on inside my body—between the virus germs and my own immune system. In a way, that's how I feel now. Sort of helpless and achy—but not physically. Does that make sense?

So I forced myself to read the redlines again tonight (as if they're my medicine). And what stood out to me was when Jesus said, "Don't pray out loud in front of everyone just to show off, but when you pray, go into your closet and pray secretly to your father in heaven. And he will hear you in private and reward you in public." Now, I'm not completely sure what all that means, but I like the idea of praying in a closet. So that's just what I did.

IN MY CLOSET
dark and silent, shoes and clothes
quiet words inside me rose
questions with no answers came

who are you and what's your name?
god, you are mysterious
but you've made me curious
riddles run all through my brain
until i fear i'll go insane
hear me now hear my prayer
answer, god, if you're there
show me how to give to you
what you want, if this is true

cm

Seven

Friday, October 11

Oh, what wonders I have to write of tonight. I almost can't hold this pen in my hand steady, for I want to dance and sing and laugh all at once. And all the time, I'm wondering, is this really me? Is this really real? Will it really last? Or is it all just a fine figment of my imagination? Am I going crazy or have I come to sanity? But, oh, I think I finally know what it means to be happy! The very word I used to despise.

What happened? What _happened?_ What makes this day so special—so outstanding from the rest?

Chloe Abigail Miller died today. R.I.P. But, don't worry, for in the same instant she returned to life too. How do I know this amazing thing really took place? I don't even know how I know exactly. I just know.

Today, I gave my heart to Jesus, and it's as if the old Chloe just melted down and sank into the soil right beneath my feet—and in her place appeared a new Chloe—a Chloe who belongs to God now. A brand-new Chloe with a whole new life ahead of her!

I must admit, even as I write these fantastic things, I almost can't believe them myself. Almost. But mostly I do. And I have a feeling that when I have doubt (and I'm guessing that's possible), God will somehow help me out.

So, this is exactly how it happened. For three days, I've been struggling with this whole thing. And even though my conversation with Laura was somewhat helpful, it also scared and disturbed me. The idea of a battle being waged for my puny, worthless little soul was a little unnerving, not to mention mind-boggling. How could the forces of the universe even know that I exist? And why should they even care? But somehow, it became clearer and clearer that they did. Still, I didn't know what to do about it.

So, today, feeling slightly like a crazed lunatic, as soon as school was out, I ran over to the cemetery—as though I couldn't get there fast enough. Once there, I just walked around, kind of dazed maybe and trying to catch my breath. I was heading to my usual spot, Katherine's old gravesite, but for some reason (a God reason!), I turned and walked in the opposite direction.

I walked up the hill to where the newer section of the cemetery is, clear to the top of the knoll. And there I found this nice, and fairly new, cement bench. I sat on it and pondered my per-

plexing situation. Maybe I was praying. I'm not
even sure. But I was bent over, and I know I was
thinking about the things Laura had said as
well as an e-mail I'd gotten from Caitlin just
last night. It had been a short message to let me
know she was coming home to visit this weekend,
but she'd also written a Bible verse at the bottom
of it. It caught my attention because she doesn't
usually do that.

So I guess I was tumbling all these various
things around in my head, and, yes, if I think
about it, I'm sure that I was praying too. But I
felt flustered and frustrated, and as I recall, I
was crying. And it felt as if I was getting
nowhere—just going round and round in circles
faster and faster, like this one particular ride at
the fair that always makes me sick. So I looked up
suddenly—wanting the ride to end—and for whatever reason (yes, a God reason!), I noticed the
gravestone directly in front of me—straight
across from the bench. It was a new-looking
headstone with shiny, white marble, and there
seemed to be a lot of writing on it. So I wiped my
tear-blurred eyes and studied it more carefully.
And to my astonishment, it was the EXACT same
Bible verse that Caitlin had written to me just
yesterday—almost word for word. This is the
verse:

"I am the way and the truth and the life.
No one comes to the Father except through me."
—Jesus Christ.

Well, it's true I've never been hit by lightning before, but that's the best way I can think to describe this feeling. It's like an electric jolt zapped right through my body and I thought: <u>This is it. This is really the truth. This is what I've been looking for.</u> And so right then and there, I did it. I asked Jesus to come into my heart.

And that's when it felt as if everything just changed in a flash. And I know, I absolutely know, I will never be the same again! Then I looked at the gravestone, curious as to who this person might be whose headstone delivered such a whopping message. And I actually recognized the name! I mean, I never really knew this guy personally, but Josh did and so did Caitlin. His name was Clay Berringer, and he was involved in their church, the same church where Allie's taking drumming lessons. I think Clay might've been related to the pastor there. But the sad part is that he was a victim of that horrible shooting incident that occurred at McFadden High a couple years back. At first, I started to feel sad, but then it hit me: Clay is all right now! Because he's with God. And, like it says on Katherine's gravestone, he's probably dancing with the angels right now. That's when I began laughing and singing and dancing right there at the top of the graveyard. And even when the clouds got all gray and heavy and it started to rain, I just kept on laughing and dancing. If anyone saw me, I know they must've thought I was crazy. But, hey, it's a good kind of crazy.

Anyway, I finally came home, soaking wet. I was kind of relieved my parents were gone (they'd already told me they had plans for the evening), and I suppose I wasn't sure if I could even explain this amazing phenomenon to anyone. I was also glad that our jam session isn't until tomorrow because I'm still not sure how I'll break the news to Allie and Laura (should I do it at the same time or separately?). But I have a feeling God's going to help me out there.

I did call Caitlin. I figured she might be at her parents' home by now, and it was worth a try to catch her. And I did. So I very calmly asked her if she could meet me for coffee tomorrow, but I didn't say anything else—not a word! I wanted her to be the first one to know about this, and I wanted to tell her in person. After all, she was kind of like my mentor.

GOD WITH A CAPITAL G
o, God, You wonderful God
You amazing, incredible, beautiful God

thank You for meeting me in the cemetery today
i didn't even know You would be there
but i'm so glad You were
and that You could care
for me
and that You could want me
for Your own
i will never be the same again
i know it—absolutely
i love You with all that i am
from the top of my head to the tip of my toes
i love You as i have never loved anyone or anything before
and yet i believe You love me
even more
cm

Eight

Saturday, October 12

What a day! What a beautiful day! Not the weather, no, that was grim and gray, and blustery. But the day was great. I started it out this morning by meeting Caitlin for coffee. She'd chosen Starbucks, and I'd forgotten to mention our new coffeehouse. But I'll never forget the look on her face when I told her what I'd done. I thought she was going to fall right off her stool. Then she jumped up and gave me a big hug and wanted to hear the whole story in detail. When I told her about doing this whole thing at Clay Berringer's grave, well, take my word for it, she was totally blown away.

And she said something that reminded me of what Laura had said. "God is up to something really big in your life, Chloe," she said in this very intense voice. "Honestly, I'm not just saying this. I believe it with my whole heart. I really do believe God is going to use you in some pretty incredible ways."

"Thanks, I hope so."

"This is just so cool, Chloe!" She was smiling big again.

I nodded. "But you know, I'm not exactly sure what I should do next."

She set down her cup. "Well, praying and reading your Bible are probably the most important things, but you also need to start having some fellowship."

"You mean like going to church?"

"Yeah, that's part of it. But you also need to get in with a group of Christian kids your own age. Is there a good youth group at your parents' church?"

I'm sure I must've frowned then. "I suppose so."

"Is there a problem?"

"Oh, I don't know." I looked down at my cappuccino. "I don't mean to sound awful, but the youth leader there, well, he's sort of, you know, kind of a yuppie type, and I just don't think I'd fit in too well."

She smiled. "Josh switched over to go to my youth group. Maybe you'd like to try it—I mean, if your parents don't mind."

I had to smile at that. "Sheesh, I think they'd be so happy to see me involved in church that they wouldn't care where I went. As long as it's not some form of a cult or something weird. In fact, I'm pretty sure my dad thought I was turning into a satanist or something equally frightening."

"Are you going to tell them?"

"Yeah, but I want to tell Josh first. Hey, did

you know he's coming home this weekend too? He should be here today."

"Nope. But I didn't get any e-mail from him this past week. I guess he's been pretty busy with school lately. Maybe you could go to church with him on Sunday."

"Yeah, that sounds like a plan."

Then we talked about some other things like her horrible roommate, and I promised that I'd be praying for her—and that things would improve. I could tell she was discouraged. And for a change I wanted to be the one to cheer her up.

"Just don't underestimate how God uses you too, Caitlin. I mean, look at what happened to me after you got involved in my life."

She laughed. "Yeah, I remember the first time I met you, and I wondered what in the world we'd possibly have in common."

I smiled. "And I'm thinking what's this preppy-looking older chick doing hanging out with the likes of me?"

"But God was really up to something."

I slowly shook my head, still amazed. It's as if this whole thing was still sinking in. "Yeah, I guess He was."

We talked and joked for about an hour before I had to head off. I'd promised my neighbor that I'd watch her baby this morning while she went grocery shopping.

"Do you like to baby-sit?" Caitlin asked as we headed out the door.

"Yeah, I think little kids are great." I didn't mention that I was motivated to add to my savings in order to purchase a new guitar and sound system.

"Then I'll have to introduce you to my aunt. She has a preschooler and a newborn baby, and she just mentioned yesterday how she's looking for a good baby-sitter, since all her old reliables took off for college this year."

"Sounds great."

So I went home and then next door to the Van Dirk's and played with Mason for a couple of hours. Hey, it's not big money, but it's kind of fun. Besides, it makes my mom happy since she and Marsha Van Dirk are pretty good friends. And by the time I came back home, Josh was here!

I waited until he'd had a good chance to visit with my parents. They were so glad to see him that I actually felt a bit jealous (but I prayed that God would help me with that), and then I realized that someday they would be happy to see me come home too. Then they decided to go to lunch.

"You coming too, sis?" Josh asked with a big smile.

I looked at my watch. "I'd like to, but I've got my friends coming over to jam today—it's a regular thing on Saturdays."

"Did you get that girl set up with Willy?"

"Yeah, she's been having lessons twice a week. He's doing it for free."

"Willy's a good guy."

"Got a minute, Josh?" I said quietly when my parents were out of earshot.

"Sure, what's up?"

"Come in here." I led him over to the library and then closed the door. "I haven't told them yet."

"Told them what? What is it?" His smile disappeared. "Is something wrong, Chloe?"

"No." I laughed. "But you'd better brace yourself."

He sat on the big leather sofa. "Okay. I'm ready."

"I did it."

"Huh?"

"I invited Jesus into my heart, Josh. I gave my life to God."

Well, he whooped like a cowboy and shot out of the chair like he had springs on his feet and grabbed me up and hugged me, then whirled me around several times before he finally set me back down. "That's the best news!" He shook his head as if he could hardly believe it and then peered at me. "Hey, you're not just pulling something over on—"

"No way! This is for real!"

Just then my parents came in. "You ready to go,

Josh?" My dad looked at us both curiously, like he suspected something was up.

"Yeah, I guess," said Josh. Then he turned back to me. "Did you tell them yet?"

"Tell us?" echoed my mom. She was behind my dad now, and I could tell by the tone of her voice that she was worried. "Tell us what? What's wrong, Chloe?"

"What's up?" my dad asked, his face concerned.

Josh looked at me and I knew it was time, but I just didn't know how to say it. Or if I even could.

"You want me to tell them?" he asked.

I nodded dumbly.

"Chloe has invited Jesus into her heart. She's become a Christian."

My parents just kind of stood there with these slightly blank expressions, like they didn't really know what to do or how to react. And now it's time for me to point something out: My parents are really nice people and law-abiding citizens and all. And they do go to church sometimes, but not regularly. And I think they consider them-selves Christians, but not in such a way that it's the most important thing in their lives (like it is with Josh and Caitlin). Or at least it's never seemed that way to me.

"That's really good news, Chloe," my dad finally said, but it was in the way that someone might react if you'd just told them you'd given up

smoking. But then he came over and gave me a hug.
I think maybe he was relieved that I hadn't done
something really frightening and horrible like
getting pregnant or hooked on acid or even getting a tattoo.

"That's nice, honey." This came from my mom.
Then she, too, stepped up and gave me a stiff
little hug. "So does this mean you'll be going to
church now?"

I looked at Josh, hoping once again for help.

"Hey, you can go to church with me tomorrow, if
you want to," he offered.

I smiled. "Sounds good to me. In fact, Caitlin
suggested the same thing."

"Caitlin?" I couldn't help but notice how his
eyes lit up.

"Yeah. She's here in town, you know."

He nodded. "Cool."

I was glad that they were all going to lunch
together and that I didn't have to go with them.
Despite everything, I do love my parents—even
more now than before—but I don't think they
understand what this really means to me. Not the
way Josh and Caitlin do. Now, if I could only think
of a way to tell Laura and Allie. Telling Laura
will be easy. But Allie? And for some reason I
knew it was important to tell them both. But how
to do it was really bugging me.

I had hoped that Laura might show up first,

but as usual, it was Allie who came early. "My mom dropped me off," she explained. "She was on her way to work, but at least I didn't have to pedal over here and get soaked on my bike."

"Great." I smiled. "I haven't had any lunch yet. You want something to eat?"

"Sure."

So as we were putting together some meat-and-cheese sandwiches, Laura arrived. "We're in the kitchen," I told her as I hung up her coat in the hall. "You hungry?"

"Yeah, I'm starved. I had to go into work early and didn't even have time to eat breakfast."

"I didn't know you have a job. Where do you work?"

"At my aunt's vet clinic. I used to just wash the animals—talk about a stinky job. But I just got moved up to the reception desk." She shook the rain off her coat. "I'm saving up for my own set of wheels."

"Cool," I said as we went into the kitchen.

"Saving for a <u>car?</u>" said Allie. "Just how old are you anyway, Laura?"

I laughed. "Didn't you know that Laura's a sophomore?"

"Yeah, I guess. But still, wouldn't that make her only fifteen?"

"I turn sixteen at the end of the month," said Laura.

"That's not fair." Allie frowned. "My birthday isn't until summer. Man, I won't be driving for like forever."

"Mine's in March," I told them. "I can't wait to get my license and a car of my own."

"Well, when I get my license and then my car, I promise to take both you young'uns for a little drive, okay?"

Allie made a face.

I glanced at Laura. I was eager to tell her my news but wasn't quite sure how to start. "You guys ready to go upstairs?" I asked.

"Can we take the rest of the food up?" asked Allie.

"Sure."

Up in the poolroom, I started picking on my guitar, just dinkin' around while they set up. Then I began playing with a song I'd started working on yesterday about how I'm changing because of Jesus.

"Is that something new?" asked Laura as she plugged in her amp.

I nodded. "Yeah, I'm still working on it."

"I like its sound," said Allie. "Not as gloomy as some of your other stuff. Why don't you teach it to us."

"Really?" I looked at Allie. "You think you'd like it?"

"Yeah, sounds like it's got a good beat."

"Okay, I'll play it and you can tell me if you still want to learn it." And so I began.

> something happened to me—
> something that might seem absurd
> something i didn't expect, like
> something that i'd never heard
> and now i'm laughin' and smilin'
> cuz my head's all rearranged
> cuz something happened to me,
> something that brought on this change
> and now i can't be the same
> i can't think the same old way
> and, ya know, I've got Jesus to blame
> cuz He entered my heart—
> He entered my heart to stay
> ya see, something's changing in me,
> my heart is open wide
> something's shining in me,
> and now I don't wanna hide
> cuz now i'm singing and dancing,
> and i've never felt so free
> cuz now i'm in love with God
> and i know that He loves me!

I stopped playing and Laura started cheering and clapping wildly, but Allie just sat there like a stone. Her face looked like she'd been punched in the stomach or eaten a bad mushroom or something.

"That's as far as I've gotten with it," I said as I rested my guitar against my leg and waited.

Then Allie whacked the cymbals with a drumstick. The loud clanging sound shattered the quiet in the room, and then she swore and hit the bass drum. "You gotta be totally kidding, Chloe!"

I shook my head. "I'm not kidding, Allie."

"No way!" She stood up now, looking big and tough despite her petite stature. And her blue eyes looked like hot flames that wanted to burn this place down to the foundation. "You cannot do this to us, Chloe! You simply cannot do this!"

"Allie," began Laura. "You don't know—"

"Do not speak to me!" She pointed her finger at Laura. "You—you are probably what's behind this whole thing. It's all your stupid fault!"

"Allie, it's not Laura's fault. Like my song says, it's Jesus' fault. It's God's fault. But, really, it's not a blame thing, it's a good thing. Honestly, I've never in my whole life been this happy before."

"Oh, you're totally deluded. Can't you see it? It's like you've been abducted by aliens and they've given you a complete lobotomy. This is not really you, Chloe. Can't you see it's all wrong?"

I laughed. "I'm sorry, but you're the one who's wrong, Allie. This is really me. This is more me than I've ever been me before. I feel as if I'm a whole person now and I like it."

"Arrgh!" Allie grabbed on to her hair like she wanted to pull it out. "I cannot believe you, Chloe! I cannot believe this! I thought you were cool. Now you've gone and done something—something like this!"

"Allie, calm down," said Laura soothingly. "Just chill, girlfriend. I want to hear what Chloe has to say."

"Fine!" Allie sank onto the drummer stool and glared at me with clenched fists, but it was like I could see a pair of angry fumes shooting out her nostrils. And she wasn't even smoking (I don't allow her to smoke in our house).

"Okay, then. Let's see. It all happened yesterday." I began. "But I guess it really started a while back..." And then step-by-step I took them through the story of my graveyard conversion, which I happen to think sounds like a great title to a song.

"That is so cool," said Laura when I finished.

Allie just growled. "Nice story, Chloe. How long did it take you to make that one up?"

"Are you serious? Do you really think I'd make something like that up?"

She shrugged, but her expression looked as if it were carved into stone. "It can't be true."

"Why not?"

"Because," she said slowly, staring into my eyes as if she thought she might be able to hypnotize me, "there is no God."

I stood there for a long time just looking at her. And really, she looked so sad and pitiful, sitting there with her borrowed drumsticks and her little-girl-lost expression, that I almost had to laugh, but thankfully I didn't. "You know, Allie," I finally said, "I used to think that exact same thing. And I guess I was almost as surprised as you when I found out I was wrong. But as your friend, I swear to you, this is the truth."

She sighed. "Maybe for you."

"But I don't see why you're taking this so hard," I continued. "I mean, it's like you're taking it so personally. Why is that?"

She shrugged again. "I don't know."

"Do you think it changes anything as far as our friendship goes?"

Without looking up she nodded.

"But why?"

She took a deep breath. "Because Christians don't hang out with witches."

"But we're friends, Allie." And to my complete surprise I went over and put my hand on her shoulder—and I have never been a touchy-feely person. It seemed kind of strange yet right, all at the same time. "And nothing is going to change that. I don't like you any less now that I'm a Christian." I paused as something occurred to me. "In fact, I think I actually like you a lot more. To be honest, I think you used to kind of scare me before."

She looked up. "I scared you?"

"Yeah. The Wicca stuff you talk about never really made sense to me, and I think it kind of scared me."

"But it doesn't now?"

"Nope."

She frowned. "Why not?"

I had to think about that for a moment. I mean, I knew it was true, but I wasn't sure how to begin to explain. Then it hit me. "Because I know that God is in me now. I know it for a fact. And I know there's nothing bigger or stronger or more loving than God."

Laura started clapping again. "Amen! You go, girl!"

I smiled. "But I still want to be friends, Allie. You're not going to dump me now that I'm a Christian, are you?"

She looked down at her lap again. "I guess not."

"Okay then. And I still want to make music."

She scowled. "Yeah, but I'll bet you'll only want to make Christian music from now on, and I can't stand that stuff."

"The truth is I don't even know what Christian music really sounds like. But I want to do music that means something to me as well as the people who hear it. And I still want to do my old songs because they're part of me, but I'd like to do some new ones too. I think it takes all of them to tell a complete story. And to me that's what music is all about—telling a story. Does that make sense?"

"I guess so."

"Are you going to be okay now?"

It almost seemed as if some of the anger had left her eyes. "Maybe. But it still feels like you pulled a fast one on me."

"Well, why don't you just hang loose and see how it plays out," I suggested.

"Yeah," Laura chimed in. "Kinda like the music. Just go with the flow and see how it sounds."

"You guys ready to do some jamming now?" I asked.

So we played for a couple of hours. And by the end, Allie seemed a little better, but she still had a kind of glazed look when we finished. Sort of shell-shocked maybe.

"You wanna ride home, Allie?" offered Laura. "My brother's here to pick me up."

"Sure," said Allie in a flat voice. "That'd be nice."

"Nice?" I whispered in her ear as I opened the door.

She almost smiled.

Poor Allie. She won't have a chance with all of us praying for her now. I know Laura is already praying for her, and probably Willy at the church too. Now I'll put Josh and Caitlin on her trail, and that poor girl won't have a chance. But won't she be glad when it's all said and done?

When Josh and my parents came home, I was perusing the classifieds again, in search of the perfect guitar. I'd circled a couple that looked promising. One sounded affordable and the other was probably too expensive.

"What are you looking for, Pumpkin?" my dad asked as he flopped down on the couch beside me.

I glanced at him curiously. He hadn't called me Pumpkin in years. "Oh, I need an electric guitar."

"An electric guitar?"

I nodded. "And an amp."

"Sounds as though you and your girlfriends are getting serious about your music."

"Yeah. We've talked about becoming a band someday, but I'm still not sure. The thing is, I can't really even jam with them with just my acoustic. I get completely drowned out."

"I can see how that could happen." He leaned over and looked at the newspaper. "So, did you find anything of interest?"

"Actually, I found a couple." I peered up at him. "And I thought I could take enough out of savings to pay for half and then maybe, uh, maybe you and Mom could..."

"Help you out?" He smiled.

I nodded. "Half on a cheap guitar isn't really too bad."

His brows lifted. "You really want a cheap guitar?"

Just then Josh came in and sat across from us. "No one wants a cheap guitar."

I laughed. "Yeah, no one wants one, but some-times she's happy to get one if that's all she can afford."

"It's a waste of money," said Josh.

Dad looked at Josh. "You know much about gui-tars?"

"I know that when we were trying to put together a band, Chris Ferris started out with a cheap guitar, and it was only a matter of weeks before he wanted to upgrade."

"Well, that makes sense to me," said Dad.

"What makes sense?" Now my mom came in and leaned against the armrest of Josh's overstuffed chair, a hand resting on his shoulder and a smile on her face. "What are we talking about?"

"Chloe wants an electric guitar," said Josh.

"What's wrong with your old guitar, honey?"

"Nothing. It's a great guitar, but it's not elec-tric, Mom. And when I jam with Laura and Allie, I get blasted away."

She nodded. I could tell she was in an exceptionally good mood since Josh was home. "I can understand that." She looked over to Dad. "You know Chloe's been really helping out around here lately and keeping her room clean."

Dad laughed. "Looks as though she's been planning this for a while."

"Actually, I had been," I confessed. "I thought I'd really work you guys too. But now that I gave my heart to God, I don't really want to manipulate anyone. Besides, I've got enough money in my savings to buy the cheap one without any help."

"Yeah, but we already decided that you should go with a good one." Josh winked at me.

"And you told me that your mother and I could go in halves with you."

"I know, but..."

"Oh, Stan, why don't we just pay for the whole thing?" Mom smiled at me. "When was the last time Chloe asked us to buy her anything?"

"That's right, I didn't cost you too much in school clothes."

Mom frowned. "Don't remind me of that, Chloe. It doesn't really work in your favor."

"Sorry."

"Have you called about these guitars yet?" asked my dad.

I stood up eagerly. "No, but I can."

"Well, Josh is right. Don't waste your time on the cheap one."

And so to make a long story short, I made the phone call, my dad wrote the check, and Josh drove me over to the ritziest neighborhood in town to pick it up. And it's so beautiful. It's a Gibson in glacier blue and in mint condition. The guy who sold it to me said that his parents had gotten it for him during a guilt trip and that he'd never even taken lessons. Now he wanted a snowboard instead. I took it up to the poolroom and plugged it right in and tried it out. It took a while to figure out, but after I got everything balanced just right, I invited Josh and my parents up and played them a couple of songs.

"Wow," said Josh. "You're really good."

My dad nodded. "I didn't realize we had a budding musician in the family."

Even my mom seemed to like it, although I could tell she thought it was too loud, but then she'd had a headache today.

All in all, it was a great day. Even the stuff with Allie can't get me down because I really think it's just a matter of time until she comes around. I even managed to get through on the phone to her tonight to tell her about my new guitar. I think it cheered her up to think we'd still jam together and hopefully sound even better than before.

i wish i knew a language
to express more adequately
my newfound appreciation
for what You've done for me
if i were a river,
i'd pour myself out
if i were a star,
i'd burst in the sky
if i were an ocean,
my waves would shout
if i were a volcano,
my lava would fly
but i am just me and all that i am
every breath every heartbeat I give
every thought every dream everything in
between
is Yours for as long as i live
i love You, God.
cm

Nine

Sunday, October 13

I went to youth group as well as church with Josh today. And while it was a little overwhelming, it was kind of fun when my brother introduced me to his friends in the youth group. Because for the first time in a long time, it felt as if he was actually sort of proud of me. That felt good.

It was different being in a church setting again, but I have to admit this church isn't like the one my parents used to drag us to when we were kids. It felt more relaxed and comfortable. And there's an assortment of people—from all walks of life. Plus I really like Pastor Tony and the youth pastor, Greg. Oh, I probably didn't agree with everything I heard today, but does anyone? I imagine I'll still question things, but, hey, I think God can handle that.

It was cool seeing Caitlin there too, with her friends Beanie and Jenny. And it was weird how they all seem so much older than before. I guess college does that to you. But it felt to me that something was slightly off between Caitlin and Josh. She appeared to be acting a little chilly

toward him. I hope they're not breaking up or anything. I know they'd never admit to anyone that
they're "involved," and I suppose they're officially
not since Caitlin believes it's wrong to date (at
least for her; she tries not to force her philosophy
on others). But I happen to know they love each
other. It's written all over their faces whenever
they're together. But today it seemed as if something was wrong. Still, I'm not worried. I know
that God is big enough to straighten them both
out if necessary (listen to me—the brand-new
Christian acting as though she knows it all!).

The pastor (Tony) is Caitlin's uncle—actually
he married Caitlin's aunt. And Caitlin introduced
me to her aunt today. Her name is Steph, and she
has a preschooler named Oliver and brand-new
baby named after Pastor Tony's deceased brother,
Clay Berringer (the same guy whose grave helped
me to find Jesus). Steph said that she's been looking for some reliable baby-sitters, and I said I'd
be glad to come whenever I can. Then she asked if
I wanted to hold her baby.

"Sure." I reached over and took him from her,
careful to support his head the way my neighbor
showed me with Mason when he was tiny. "He's so
small," I said to Steph.

She smiled. "He's grown almost a pound
already."

I looked into his big dark blue eyes and

thought it's almost like you could see God or eternity or something just incredibly amazing in there. But I didn't say those words out loud. I'm sure it would've sounded strange, and I didn't want Steph to think I was too weird. I mean, I'm not exactly sure how Christians are supposed to act. And in some ways I'm not even sure that I care, because I don't want to <u>act</u> like anything. I just want to <u>be</u>. Besides, I wasn't even totally sure what I was thinking at the time, something sort of indescribable. But there was definitely something beautiful in that little boy's eyes.

Even now I'm wondering, does God see something like that in my eyes? In everyone's? Does He look into our eyes and see something that's so far beyond what we can begin to dream or imagine that it would just totally blow us away if we could see it for ourselves? I don't know, but it's something to ponder. And it seems as though there's so much to ponder these days. It's like my mind's been opened wide to all the wonders around me. Like I'm seeing God's hand in almost everything, and it's so cool. I think about how pessimistic and negative I used to be. I used to make fun of almost everything. But now it's like there's such life and possibility all around me. How could I have ever been so down before? Except, of course, I didn't have God. He makes all the difference.

WHAT CHANGED?
I've gone through the looking glass
to find everything right side up
to see what appeared empty
is now an overflowing cup
the sky that loomed so cloudy
now glows with rainbow bright
the sun now warm and golden
erases gloom of night
my world before was hopeless
shackled, i wasn't free
now i soar like an eagle
and all that has changed is me
thank You, God!
cm

Monday, October 21

Last week started out so great, and for the first several days it felt like I was walking on clouds—high above the ordinary stuff that had dragged me down so much before. But by Thursday, I started feeling as if I was coming back down to earth some. And it was a little disappointing.

I guess it started with Tiffany Knight. Okay, I realize I'm supposed to love my enemies, and that I can't do it without Jesus' help. But the truth is, I just felt fed up with her today. She says the cruelest things. Not just to me, but to anyone who catches her eye (for being different). And she threw one of her nasty little jabs at Marty Ruez, an overweight girl who's in choir. I won't even dignify Tiffany's remark by quoting her. But it was mean to the bone.

I'd been actually trying to smile at Tiffany and her thugs lately. And, man, is that ever a challenge—it'd be easier to swallow ground glass. Not just because of who they are, although that's enough right there, but also because I've never been a real smiley-type person in the first place.

Okay, in all fairness, maybe I was before I started dressing and acting differently. But now with the way I look, it totally conflicts. Which brings me to another problem: the way I look. Some people (I mean, primarily my parents and maybe some Christians who shall remain unnamed) are acting as though now that I'm a Christian I should start to look different. But I don't really get that. I think the way I look is sort of useful for linking me to all sorts of people who normally get left out. You know, the outsiders or "total misfits," as people like Tiffany call them. Well, it's as if my appearance makes me accessible to those people. And I like that. Besides, I have absolutely no desire to start dressing like Tiffany and her kind. So what am I supposed to do? Anyway, I'm praying about this. I figure God knows what's best for me. And I want to get it straight from Him.

Now back to feeling bummed because I got mad at Tiffany and wanted to punch her face in and suddenly questioned whether I'm a very good Christian or not. I could tell that I was starting to get depressed and all heavy, but instead of giving in to it, the way I used to do, I took a walk during lunch and just talked it all out with God. And by fifth period I felt better. The next day I told Laura about the whole thing and asked if she ever felt like that.

"Oh, yeah," she said as we walked to the cafeteria. "All the time. I mean, just 'cuz you invite God into your life doesn't mean your troubles go away. But sometimes people think that, especially right at first, and that can get you down if you let it."

I waited for her to get a tray. "But why is that? Why should it get us so down?"

"Probably 'cuz you're feeling so good at first and you just want to keep feeling like that forever."

I nodded. "Yeah, and why shouldn't you?"

She laughed. "Because it's impossible."

"Why's that? I thought God could do anything." I frowned as I picked up a chef's salad.

"You mean like keeping you on a constant high—like you're taking uppers or something?"

"Sort of." I noticed a cafeteria worker listening to us then, looking all worried as if she thought we were talking about drugs. I smiled at her and said, "Don't worry, we're not talking about speed; we're talking about God." And she just laughed. So we waited until we were seated to finish this conversation.

"So, are you saying God can't keep us feeling good all the time?" I asked as I bit into a carrot stick.

"I'm sure He could. But I doubt that He will. Life's not supposed to be like that—even when you're a Christian. It's more like an up-and-down and round-and-round kind of thing, like a roller coaster, you know?" She rolled her eyes up and down dramatically. "You like the roller coaster?"

"Sure."

"And would you like it if it just went straight like a train?"

I laughed. "Probably not."

"Maybe life's supposed to be like that too. Up and down, exciting and challenging and never predictable. Just make sure that it's God who's directing your ride."

I nodded. "I guess that makes sense."

"We still on to jam this Saturday?"

"Yeah, but I have to quit at five sharp to go baby-sit."

"That's cool."

And so anyway, that helped me put things in a better perspective. Life's not supposed to be a smooth ride—it's supposed to be bumpy. Okay, I can handle that. And with people like Tiffany Knight, combined with the guilt trip Allie's laying on me lately, not to mention the daily teasing that Jake and Cesar and Spencer like to dish out about me turning into a "Jesus Freak" (their favorite nickname for me right now), it does feel a little rocky and bumpy.

Some people might wonder why I don't drop my slightly freaky friends, especially when they're giving me grief for my belief. But that's just the reason: because they are my slightly freaky friends. I really believe I'm supposed to hang in there with them and just be myself. Only now I can actually love them better than before—and even accept them for who they are (drugs and problems and dragon tattoos to boot). I mean, isn't that what Jesus did for me?

And as I continue to read my redlines in the Bible, I'm finding that He did exactly that same thing with almost everyone. Well, except for some of those cranky old "religious" guys—particularly the scribes and Pharisees who acted as though they were better than everyone else. And I sure don't want to be like a "religious" person and start acting or thinking I'm better than anyone else, no matter who they are or how they look or act—even if they're Tiffany Knight. But I'm starting to realize that not all Christians think like this. And this bugs me.

WHAT'S UP, GOD?
what's up with looking down on others?
aren't we all just sisters, brothers?
why make clubs and bands and cliques?
why build walls or pull mean tricks?
why paste fake smiles on a face
when love that's real is wrapped in grace?
what's up with acting all superior?
like you're as clean as your exterior?
Jesus called them filthy graves—
For He's the only One who saves
us from insecurity
only He gives purity
make me clean, Jesus
amen
cm

Tuesday, October 22

Laura called me tonight and said, "I need to talk to you about something important."

"What's up?"

"It's about Allie."

"What's wrong?" I sat on my bed to brace myself. "Did something bad happen to her?"

"No, that's not it. But I'm feeling like it's wrong for me to be hanging with her so much."

Now, to be honest, I'd been expecting something like this for some time now. Laura had been dropping hints for the past couple weeks. But then she'd always add something like, "But I'm really praying for her to get saved." As if that made it okay to dis her.

"Wrong to be <u>with</u> her?" I repeated, hoping she might hear how she sounded (at least to me).

"Yeah, our pastor's been preaching about how the light isn't supposed to mix with the darkness and how we need to stay away from evil."

"Yeah?"

"And Allie is obviously involved in evil."

"Yeah?"

"And so I feel like I'm supposed to stay away from her."

"You feel like this is what God's telling you to do, Laura?"

"Yes. It seems right."

"I guess I can't argue with that. Only you know what God's telling you to do. But just so you know, that's not what He's telling me to do."

"What's He telling you?"

I laughed. "Actually, I haven't really heard His voice. Have you?"

"Not in an audible sort of way, but I think He speaks through my pastor. What do you think God

wants you to do, Chloe? Do you really think it's
right to be such good friends with, you know,
someone like Allie?"

"I'm still figuring these things out. I mostly
just go by my redlines—that and what I hear at
church."

"And?"

"My redlines show me that Jesus was good
friends with all kinds of people—even though a
lot of them seemed like total losers. And the
religious people actually accused Him of hanging out with sinners since a lot of them were
prostitutes or thieves or whatever. And Jesus told
those guys that He came to heal the sick and feed
the hungry."

"Yeah, but He was Jesus."

"That's true. But He also told us to do like He
did."

Now the phone line grew silent. "I still don't
know..." She sighed. "It's pretty confusing."

"Hey, I'm not telling you what to do, Laura. I'm
just telling you where I'm coming from. I'm not
afraid of Allie and her witchy problems. And I'm
not afraid of Spencer and Jake with their drug
problems. If God told me to quit being friends
with them, well, I guess I'd have to do it. But at
the same time, I'd have to wonder what kind of God
I'm serving if He doesn't want me to follow Jesus'
example."

"But what about the whole darkness and light thing?"

I thought about that for a minute. I went over and turned off the light in my room. Naturally, it got really dark. Then I turned it back on. I just cracked up laughing.

"What?" demanded Laura. "What are you laughing at?"

"Are you in your bedroom right now?"

"Yes, why?"

"Okay, do something for me, will you? Close the door and then turn off the lights, all of them." I waited for a few seconds.

"Okay, I did it. And now I'm standing here in the dark. Are you happy?"

"Right. Now turn one light back on."

"Okay. I did."

"What happened to the dark, Laura?"

"Uh...it's gone."

"Right. Now what happened to the darkness when you turned off the light?"

I heard her gasp. "Oh, man, I think I get it!"

"Yeah, that's exactly what I thought too. If we remove ourselves from that so-called darkness, then what's left?"

"Just darkness."

"And excuse me for sounding so elementary, but why did Jesus come to earth?"

"To bring light?"

"Well then?"

"I guess I'm going to be thinking about this some more."

"Good night, Laura. I love you!"

"I love you too, Chloe. Will you forgive me for acting like such a total bozo sometimes?"

"Oh, Laura, don't say that. You're one of the wisest people I know."

"Sheesh, then you should start hanging out with some better peop—" She stopped. "Well, bite my tongue. There I go again. Good night, Chloe."

After I hung up the phone, I thought about our conversation, and I can honestly say I've never had that exact thought before (about turning the light off and seeing the darkness take over). God had to have been the one to show me that. And that feels pretty exciting.

chase away my darkness with Your Light
fill my life with love that shines so bright
that it's clear what's good and right and true
so when folks look at me, they'll see You
amen
cm

Wednesday, October 23

I remembered that Laura's sixteenth birthday is this upcoming weekend. So during lunchtime, while she was in the rest room, I asked some of her friends if anyone had made any plans, and everyone said no. So I asked one of her best friends, LaDonna Denney, "Do you think anyone would mind if I gave Laura a party?"

LaDonna shrugged, but she almost seemed irritated by my question. "I guess not. But how would you know who to invite?"

I smiled. "Maybe you could help me out."

She softened a little. "Yeah, I guess so. Is it supposed to be a surprise party?"

"I think that'd be fun. We usually jam together on Saturdays anyway, so maybe we could just have the party afterward. Hey, maybe you guys could sneak into my house while we're jamming and set things up. We make so much noise we wouldn't even hear you."

"Yeah." LaDonna's eyes lit up. "And then maybe you guys could play some for us. Laura keeps talking like you're all really hot and everything."

"I wouldn't say we're hot. But I guess we're okay, for beginners that is." I looked at my watch. "I'll check with my mom to make sure Saturday night is okay. Can you start putting together a list or something?"

"What about boys?"

"Huh?"

"Is it just a girl party or are we inviting boys too?"

I could see Laura coming our way. "You decide, LaDonna." Then I headed back to my freak friends' table. I like to spread myself around.

"Okay," she called out.

So I phoned my mom at work to ask about the party.

"Sure, I don't see why not." Then she paused. "Uh, you're not talking about a _wild_ party are you?" She lowered her voice. "There wouldn't be any alcohol or drugs or anything like that would there?"

I laughed. "Not if I can help it. And I promise to clean up everything afterward."

"Well, okay, then. I like Laura, and I think that sounds like a nice idea."

So, it was settled. We're throwing Laura a surprise party. And LaDonna slipped me a note in the hallway. It said, "no boys," and I was kind of relieved. I knew that if we included boys, I'd have to invite my few guy friends, and then I'd have to make it clear that there was to be no drinking or drugs and, with them, well, there's just no guarantees. So I was glad.

Later that day, Allie came over to practice on the drums. After about an hour, I went up and joined her. I'm still learning a lot about my new guitar, and it's fun to practice with real drums. "That was great," I said when we finally stopped and I pulled the plug on my amp.

"So are you staying later on Saturday for the surprise party?" I asked kind of tentatively since I've noticed how Allie seems to be keeping a cool distance between her and Laura lately. For some reason she has more of a problem with Laura being a Christian than she does with me. But Allie's clearly not happy with either of us. And she's not afraid to tell me whenever she feels like it.

"What are you going to do at your party?" she asked with a bored expression. "Play pin the tail on the donkey? Or maybe spin the bottle and then, since boys aren't allowed, we can kiss each other?" She laughed. "Girls are always kissing each other lately, and on the lips too—"

"Gross! What girls?"

"You know, in the movies. It's the latest, haven't you seen it?"

I made a face. "Look, I might love you, Allie, but not like that. And don't get any weird ideas about kissing any girls at Laura's party either."

"Oh, you've gotten so narrow since you became the good little Christian girl."

I laughed. "For your info, I never would've kissed you before I was a Christian either. Sheesh, I wouldn't even tell you I loved you back then. Hey, I've come a long way, baby!" And I know this is true. It's funny how I feel so much more relaxed and at ease now. I used to sort of watch

every word I said, every step I took, trying to create this image of who I thought I wanted to be.
Now I just want to be who God wants me to be. It's
a lot more fun.

But Allie still didn't look convinced. "If you
ask me, an all-girl birthday party sounds pretty
dull."

"It doesn't have to be."

She rolled her eyes at me. "Well, what are we
going to do at this party? Light candles and sing
'Kumbaya'?"

Now I was getting a little irritated by her
put-downs. And I sort of slipped up—okay, I
really slipped up. "Hey, you'd probably get into
the candle lighting thing, wouldn't you, Allie?
Isn't that what the secret coven does at their
witch meetings?"

"I don't know," she snapped. "It's not like I've
ever been to one."

"Why not?" Now, don't ask me why I suddenly
started going down this foolish trail. Let's just
say my mouth was running way ahead of my brain
and my heart.

"Because, if you really need to know, I've
never been invited."

"So, what's the deal? Are the other witches all
snooty or something? Do you have to qualify to be in
their special club? Or do you have to get a special
gown or some magic potion or something?"

That's when Allie started crying, and then I felt totally wicked.

"I'm sorry, Al. I don't know why I said all that. Please, forgive me. I'm really, really sorry."

She sniffed but didn't answer.

"Allie?" my mom called up the stairs. "Your mom's here to pick you up."

"I gotta go."

"I'm really sorry," I said again. "That was so stupid—"

"See ya." And she took off down the stairs.

Right now I feel like a total noodle-brained, jerk-head ignoramus. I've already prayed and asked God to forgive me. And I've tried to call Allie about a hundred times, but as usual her line's always busy. I wonder if they don't just leave that thing off the hook. Anyway, I can see how easy it is to fall into that old pharisee trap. Sheesh, I'm as bad as anyone. What right did I have to say those things or to be so judgmental? I know that's <u>not</u> what Jesus would do. I mean, it's not as if He'd tell her it was okeydoke to be a witch, but He sure wouldn't tease or pick on her. And He would definitely love her. Somehow, I'll try to patch it up with her tomorrow.

EYES WIDE SHUT
let me see myself as i really am
just a stumbling, bumbling fool

foot in my mouth, a stupid ham
spitting out words incredibly cruel
help me, o God, to understand
the way that You want me to live
cover me now in Your gracious hand
i beg you, Lord Jesus, forgive
amen
cm

Ten

Friday, October 25

Try as I might, I can't seem to patch things up with Allie. And it sure doesn't help that she's not talking to me. I asked her if she was coming over today to practice drums, and she just gave me "the look." The look is when she narrows her eyes and tightens her facial features and basically tries to freeze you up with an icy stare. It's pretty intense and I wonder if she isn't chanting some kind of secret witch spell in her head, although she's told me over and over that her witchcraft isn't to hurt but to help. Still, I wonder. Not that she scares me, because really she doesn't. Mostly I feel sorry for her because she seems so lost most of the time. And now I've gone and alienated her.

I'm really praying that God will help me break through to her. For some reason it seems like an important friendship. I'm sure music has something to do with it, and she's really gotten pretty good on the drums. But there's more too. And it makes me sad to think I could be losing her as a friend. Even Cesar seemed concerned at lunch today.

"What's the deal with you two?" he asked me after Allie stormed off.

"I said something stupid."

He leaned forward with interest. "What?"

"Oh, I kinda made fun of her witchcraft thing, and it hurt her feelings."

He laughed. "Hey, we make fun of you and your Christian thing all the time, and you seem to take it pretty well."

I smiled. "Yeah, well, maybe that's because 'my Christian thing' has made me a lot happier than the way I used to be."

"Yeah, I've kinda noticed."

We were the only ones at the table now, and it was almost time to go to class. But for some reason I felt I was supposed to say something. I just wasn't sure what. So I asked God (silently, of course) to help me. "Yeah, I wasn't enjoying life too much before."

"You were a pretty gloomy girl."

I laughed. "It's like everything just seemed so hopeless and futile and basically cruddy to me."

"And now it doesn't?"

"No. Now it's like everything's different. But I realize that I'm the one who's changed."

"My mom's pretty into religion. She goes to Mass all the time and would never dare to miss her precious confession. But I haven't been inside the doors of the church for years. It really makes her mad."

"Well, the truth is, I'm not too crazy about the whole religion thing myself."

He looked puzzled.

"I mean, I'm still not sure what the purpose is for all these church denominations, or why they're all different and why some don't get along with others. I think that's pretty weird, and I'd really like to know what God thinks about the whole thing."

"I never thought of it like that—like what would God think."

"I just don't think it's what Jesus intended," I said.

"What do you think He intended?"

"I think He'd like for us all to just live like He did."

Just then the warning bell rang and Cesar picked up his backpack. "I'll get kicked out of algebra if I'm late again, but you know, I'd really like to continue this conversation. You wanna get together for a Coke after school or something?"

"Sure, I'll meet you out front."

So we met after school and walked down to the McDonald's that's nearby and sat in the corner to talk some more. "You probably shouldn't take anything I tell you too seriously," I warned him.

"I mean, it makes sense to me, but then what do I know? I've only been a Christian for a couple of weeks now."

"But what you were saying about religions makes sense to me. One of the reasons I quit going to church is because I got sick of all the rules. I mean, why does it have to be so complicated?"

"I don't know. It seems like if we do things God's way, it should be simple. And His way is to believe in Jesus and invite Him into our life. Other than that, I'm not reading much in my Bible that talks about churches or denominations or any of that stuff. Of course, I'm only reading the words that Jesus said."

"What kind of Bible do you have?"

I laughed. "It's a regular one. But it has all of Jesus' words written in red. A friend of mine suggested I just read those to start out. And so that's what I've been doing. And it seems pretty straightforward. Jesus mostly talks about simple stuff like treating other people right and forgiving others and helping the poor and loving God with your whole heart—stuff like that."

He nodded. "Well, I could probably get into that. It's just all the other rules and regs that mess me up."

We talked a little longer then he had to leave for work. He's gotten on at Home Depot like he'd hoped and is working about twenty hours a week now. "It was good to talk about this, Chloe," he said as we parted ways. "It gives me something to think about."

"Cool." I waved and headed toward the bus stop.

WHY, WHY, WHY?
why do we make complications
full of foolish implications?
why the choice to convolute
when all it serves is to dilute?
what is real and right and true?
just love Jesus—He loves you
why so many denominations?
legal dogma, rules, citations
wall us in and breed more fear
conform or you are outta here!
why not choose simplicity
and turn from our duplicity
love and learn to forgive
Jesus, show us how to live
amen
cm

Sunday, October 27

Laura was totally blown away by her surprise party yesterday. And it turned out pretty cool if I do say so myself. To my surprise, even Allie showed up. Although she was still wearing a highly visible chip on her shoulder. Just the same she was civil to Laura, even if she was decidedly chilly toward me. I have a feeling that the only reason she came was so it wouldn't look as if she had boycotted Laura. I don't think Allie wanted to look like the bad guy. She left before anyone else and somehow managed to avoid saying more than a few words to me. But I was glad she came. And I hope that means she's softening up a little.

I'll have to admit the highlight of the evening (for me anyway) was when everyone crowded into the poolroom and we played a couple songs for them. They just clapped and cheered like we were the greatest. Then everyone kept saying how we should cut a CD. As if! But who knows? Maybe someday.

Laura found me in the kitchen as things were drawing to an end, and her eyes were just gleaming. "Chloe, this was so great! No one ever threw me a surprise party before."

I smiled and rinsed some sticky frosting from my hands. "Well, then I'd say it was about time."

"I was surprised that Allie showed up after the way she's been giving you the chill-out lately."

"Yeah, me too. I guess her coming has more to do with you than me since she barely spoke to me, as I'm sure you noticed while we were jamming."

"I was wondering if she was ready to dump us both."

"I hope not. I think I'll try to get together with her tomorrow and see if we can't hammer this thing out. I don't think I can take another week of her being mad at me."

"Good luck, Chloe. I'll be praying for you."

So today after church, I called Allie, and amazingly her phone rang and she picked it up. "Can we get together and talk?" I asked, hoping she wasn't about to hang up on me. I wouldn't put it past her.

"About what?"

"About this whole thing—about being friends."

"Friends?" I could hear the skeptical tone in her voice.

"Yeah, despite what you think, I'd still like to be friends."

She didn't say anything for a while. Then finally, "Okay, I guess we could talk. "

"Do you want to meet somewhere?"

"I can't. I'm baby-sitting."

"Baby-sitting?"

"Yeah, my little brother."

"I didn't even know you had a little brother, Allie. "

"Yeah, well, there's a lot you don't know about me."

"How old is he?"

"Eight."

"What's his name?"

"David."

"So is it okay if I come over?"

"Sure, whatever."

I knew the general location of her apartment complex but had to ask for specific directions. Then I hopped on my bike and headed over. It was a pretty run-down complex, and their apartment was located on the first floor directly in front of a parking lot that some of the kids were using as a makeshift playground. I knocked on the door and waited for her to answer.

She opened the door and said, "Come on into my palace," in a very sarcastic tone.

The apartment looked tiny with a kitchen and living room crammed into less space than my entire bedroom. But what caught my eye was the little boy sitting on the floor. I could tell right off by the almond shape of his eyes and the size of his head that he probably had Down's syndrome. I have a second cousin with the same thing. Her name is Katy and she's a little sweetheart.

"You must be David." I knelt by the boy.

He looked up and smiled then held out a wooden block in his little hand, as if he wanted me to take it.

"Thanks." I said, sitting next to him. "What're you building here?"

"House."

So I stacked my red block on top of his yellow one, and then he clapped his hands together.

"You don't have to do that, Chloe," said Allie in an exasperated voice.

I looked up at her. "I know that." Then I picked up another block and set it on the others, and he clapped again and then handed me another. I set it on top, then handed him one. "Now your turn. "

Slowly, he set the block on top. The stack teetered but didn't fall, and now I clapped my hands. "Good job, David." Next he handed me a green block, but when I placed it on top, the whole thing toppled and David's eyes grew wide. But I just clapped my hands and laughed. "Kaboom! "

"Kaboom!" he said.

Allie sat on the couch and leaned forward, her elbows on her knees and her chin in her hands. "So, did you come all the way over here just to play with David?"

"Maybe." I stacked my block on his again and waited.

"Well, now that you've seen my mansion, I'm sure you've got better things to do than hang around here."

I turned and looked at her. "Allie, I'm sorry I said those things to you. Will you please forgive me and give me another chance to be your friend?"

She shrugged. "I don't know why you even want to be friends."

"What do you mean?"

"We're like totally different. And I figure you'll dump me sooner or later anyway. Maybe sooner is just better."

"I don't know why you think I'll dump you." I stacked another block.

She shrugged again. "Because that's what usually happens." She waved her arms. "I mean, look at how I live. Me and my mom and David all crammed into this cruddy little apartment. My dad's not even paying child support most of the time, and my mom's barely scraping by working as a clerk at Albertsons. Not exactly your Lifestyles of the Rich and Famous."

"You know... I've told you over and over, I don't care about that."

She leaned over and looked directly into my eyes. "Well, I do!"

"That's your problem." I put another block on, watching as the tower teetered.

"That's right!" She stood now and walked into the kitchen. "That's my problem. And all I have are problems, problems, problems. My life is just one great big problem!"

"Just because you don't have money doesn't mean you have to have problems." I watched as the tower tumbled again, and this time David said, "Kaboom!"

"How would you know?" Her voice was so loud that David's eyes grew wide, and he seemed slightly frightened.

"Hey, you want to turn down the volume for the sake of your little brother here?"

She looked over the counter at me and sighed. "Sorry, Davie."

"Allie, I'm sorry you guys don't have a lot of money. But it's not the end of the world. And I'd still like to be friends with you if you'd just—"

"But what about Wicca? I know that you hate my being involved in it."

I stood up now. "I have never said that."

"But I can tell."

"Well, maybe I just don't get it, Allie. I can't see how Wicca is making your life any better. And frankly you don't seem too happy to me."

"You mean just because you're on this whole 'I'm so happy to be a Christian' trip."

I shrugged. "Hey, it works for me."

"Does it really?" She was studying me closely now, as if she was looking for something wrong, some flaw or imperfection she could point out and pick at.

"I'm not saying life's perfect. But something is definitely different inside of me. Something that was broken or empty or missing or whatever isn't anymore. When I asked God into my life, something changed. I mean, really changed. I guess maybe you can't see it. Or maybe you don't want to see it. Or you don't like it. But I am different, Allie. I know it. I feel it. I believe it."

"It's just unfair!" She whacked her fist onto the counter making a coffee mug jump.

"Unfair?" I shook my head.

"You have it all. You have rich parents—two of them actually living together! And you have normal brothers—"

"Well, at least one."

"And you're a great musician, and you want a new guitar and Daddy dearest just goes out and buys you one. And then you decide it's cool to become a Christian, and so you do and you make it look like that's all easy and great—"

"Hey, wait a minute. You can paint this thing any way you want, but that doesn't make it so. My life hasn't been all perfectly wonderful. I was so messed up last year that my parents considered sending me to a private reform school. My older brother is strung out on drugs. My parents both work and have such active social lives that I hardly ever see them. It's only recently that I've even felt like they love me, and even that feels a little conditional. So don't start acting as if everything's all peachy-keen as far as my life goes. I know your life's not the greatest, but it could get better if you'd let it."

"Let it?" She laughed. "Just idly sit by and see what's coming my way next?"

"That's not what I mean."

"Well, the reason I got into Wicca was so that I could take some control over my rotten little life—so I could make some changes and actually get somewhere."

"And is it working?"

"I thought it was working, at first, when I started getting involved with you and into music. That was the first really good thing that had happened to me in ages."

I thought about that. "Okay, I don't want to step on your toes here, but will you hear me out? First of all, I didn't become friends with you because of Wicca. In fact, it used to really weird me out that you were involved in it. And if I hadn't become a Christian, I probably would've dropped out of our friendship by now.

"Second, getting into drumming. My brother Josh has pretty much given you that drum set, but if he thought for one minute that you thought it was because of Wicca, he'd take it right back. Believe me, I know him well enough to know that's true. He's a pretty conservative Christian, and he wouldn't like being connected to anything that has to do with witchcraft.

"Third, your free drumming lessons are from a

Christian guy who's got a good and generous heart. And that also has absolutely nothing to do with Wicca. So, for you to go around giving witch-craft all the credit for the music thing—well, that's just plain ludicrous."

She didn't say anything.

"In fact, if you think Wicca has anything to do with your music, then you probably shouldn't even want to be playing with me and Laura since you know we're both Christians. Wouldn't it upset your karma or whatever it is you call it?"

Her head was hanging down now, and I realized that I'd probably, once again, gone too far. "Look, Allie, I'm sorry if what I'm saying hurts your feelings. That's not my intent. I'm just trying to tell you the truth."

She looked up at me and she was crying again. Now I felt totally rotten. What was wrong with me anyway? "I'm sorry, Allie." And then I started to cry too. "Man, I don't know why I let my mouth just take off like that again. Honestly, I didn't mean to hurt you."

She shook her head. "No, it's okay."

"It's not okay." I glanced over to see if we were upsetting David, but he seemed to be absorbed in stacking his blocks. "The point is, I want to be your friend, and I wish you'd quit pushing me away." I stepped toward her thinking I should probably give her a hug, but somehow I just couldn't. This is something I think I need to work on. "I'm sorry I made you cry."

Now she stepped back and looked at me. I was afraid she was going to yell and tell me to leave, but instead she smiled and wiped her eyes on a kitchen towel. "What you said about Wicca probably was true. I guess I just haven't looked at it that way."

I blinked and then took the towel and wiped my own eyes. "Really?"

"Yeah." She sighed. "I hadn't thought about the whole drumming thing like that. But you're right. It didn't have anything to do with Wicca. How could it? And you're also right that getting into Wicca hasn't made me any happier. To be honest, it's pretty frustrating. It's like I have to have money to buy the stuff to do the things and, well, I just don't. But the reason I got so involved with it to start with was because I felt like I have no control over—" she waved her arms—"any of this. It's like life just keeps getting worse and worse, and it plows right over me and takes me along with it. And I was fed up."

"I know how you feel."

"Last summer, I started using the computer at the library while David was at story hour, and the woman next to me was visiting all these Wicca websites. She told about how it was a great way to get some control over your life—and it just sounded so good to me. So I would go in there and read everything I could. And then school started and it seemed as if maybe things were going to change for me. Then I met you and they did."

"Okay, can I be gut-level honest with you right now, Allie?"

"Sure, why not."

"Well, I really believe that our meeting and becoming friends was not an accident."

She nodded. "Yeah, me too."

"And I believe the whole music thing wasn't an accident either."

She nodded more vigorously this time. "Me too."

"I think God is behind the whole thing. I haven't actually said this out loud before, but I really think He wants us to do something big with our music. I know it seems crazy, but I really believe it—" I tapped on my chest—"in here."

She just stared at me. "But I don't get it."

"What?"

"If God is doing this thing, then why would He involve me?"

I laughed. "Why not? I happen to think you're pretty cool. You've been a good friend. You're a good drummer. But mostly I think it's because God really loves you, Allie. Can't you see that?"

She didn't say anything.

"Look, I'm not going to pressure you into giving your heart to God, but it's sure changed my life. And I hope you can trust that I wouldn't lie to you about this whole thing. Would I?"

She studied me. "No, I don't think you would."

"So would you just consider what I'm saying?"

She finally nodded. "I guess I already am."

"Great. Well, I better go now. I've got a pile of homework to do, and I want to be able to go to church tonight." I headed for the door.

"Chloe?"

"Yeah."

"Do you think I could come with you?"

"To church?"

"Yeah."

"Sure. Of course!"

And so, Allie went to church with me tonight. No, she didn't walk down the aisle and give her heart to Jesus. But she told me that she wants to learn more about being a Christian.

"I'm not making any promises," she said as we went out to the parking lot. She quickly lit and smoked a cigarette as we waited for my dad to pick us up. "But I'll look into it—just like I was looking into Wicca."

"So are you still looking into Wicca too?"

"I'm not sure. Maybe I'll have to see which one of these—if either—works for me."

"Sounds fair."

o, God, tell her that You love her
show her that Your way
is better—best!
put Your arms around her
and tell her she's special
show her that You have
better things in store
give her hope
and ignite her faith
so that she can love You
more than anything!
amen
cm

Eleven

Thursday, October 31

What a totally weird night! In fact, I'm still not completely sure what's going on. Okay, let me back up a little and start at the beginning. It all began yesterday when I got a call from Mike from the Paradiso Café.

"I listened to your demo," he said in a matter-of-fact voice.

"Yeah?" I waited with pounding heart, barely able to breathe.

"And it's pretty good."

"Really?" I felt the air return to my lungs. "You liked it?"

"Yeah. And I thought, maybe if you're not busy tomorrow night—do you already have plans?"

"Busy? No, no. It's not like I was going trick-or-treating or anything." I laughed nervously.

"Yeah, I didn't think so. Maybe you'd like to come do some songs then. Like around eight?"

"Sure." Well, I was so happy you'd think someone had offered me a multimillion-dollar recording contract. But I tried to contain myself as I went down to tell my parents. And maybe I contained myself too well, because they just said stuff like "that's nice" and "sounds like fun." Acting as if these things happen to me all the time. But the next day at school, I got a better reaction from Laura, who actually screamed in the hallway.

"You're kidding!" Then she hugged me and promised to come watch.

Now, that was satisfying.

Then I told Allie the good news while we were waiting in the lunch line.

"Really? You're going to play at Paradiso?" She looked at me with obvious admiration. Well, at first anyway. Then she sort of frowned. "All by yourself?"

"Yeah." I nodded as I picked up a Jell-O. "Remember I told you how I took in a demo tape a while back. It was before we'd even started jamming or anything."

"And so you're going to go solo then?"

The way she said the word solo sounded like it was comparable to bungee jumping or motorcycle racing without a helmet. "Yeah." I filled my soda cup.

"And you're okay with that?"

"Sure." I turned to look at her. "Why wouldn't I be?"

She scowled. "Oh, no reason. It's just that I thought we were a band or something." Now her tone was decidedly sarcastic. And she looked like

I'd stabbed her in the back or cheated from her homework when she wasn't looking.

"Look, Allie, it's not like I'm leaving you guys out of anything. This is something totally different. The Paradiso isn't even set up for bands yet. And besides, we're not really even a real band. And we're sure not ready for a real gig. I mean, we don't even have a name or anything."

"Yeah, sure." She set her tray on the table then turned to Jake and Cesar who were already eating. "Chloe's got her first music gig tonight," she said in a flat tone.

"Really?" Cesar's eyes lit up. "Where is it?"

"The Paradiso." She sat down and sighed deeply. "And she didn't even invite her band to play with her."

"Allie," I tried again. "It's not like that. The coffeehouse is not set up to—"

"Yeah, yeah." She waved her hand. "I think you're just embarrassed to be seen with us amateurs."

"I am not!"

"What time is the gig?" asked Cesar.

"At eight." I smiled. "You guys should come."

"You mean instead of trick-or-treating?" Jake pretended to pout. "You really expect us to give up the goodies just to hear the Jesus Freak play?"

I laughed. "Yeah, and I'll bet you guys really go trick-or-treating too."

"Well, there's more than one kind of trick-or-treating, ya know." He winked at me like he'd just told a dirty joke.

"Hey, you can count me in, Chloe," said Cesar. "I'll be at the Paradiso."

I turned to Allie and put on my best pleading face. "Won't you come too?"

She still looked unhappy.

"Laura was okay with this," I continued. "She said she's going to come, and you could probably hitch a ride with her."

Allie sniffed. "You know Halloween is important to—"

Jake laughed. "Oh, yeah, Allie, are you going to be hanging out with a bunch of witches and worshiping the devil and stuff?"

She glared at him. "It's not like that!"

"I thought you said you were giving all that Sabrina, the Teenage Witch stuff up," said Cesar.

I remained silent. I hadn't talked to Allie about her Wicca thing since our conversation at her house last Sunday, and I guess I'd just hoped that she was losing interest. Although now it didn't seem like it.

"I never said I was giving anything up," she snapped. Then she turned and glared accusingly at me as if I was the one who had spread these rumors.

"Hey, don't look at me." I held my hands up. "I didn't say anything."

"You're the one who said it, Allie," Jake reminded her. "Remember when I asked you about putting a hex on my stepmom the other day, and you said you weren't into that stuff anymore?"

She shrugged. "Well, that's not how it works anyway."

I could tell she was upset about that whole coffeehouse thing, so I didn't say anything until it was almost time to go to class. By then the guys had departed and it was just the two of us.

"Hey, I'm really sorry the whole band can't play at the Paradiso tonight, but don't you want to come anyway? I could really use some support in the audience. And besides, if it goes over well tonight, maybe I can see about having the band play there another time. It's not like we three girls would really take up a lot of space. And I suppose we could turn our amps down a little."

"Really?" Her eyes brightened. "That'd be so cool."

"And Laura said she'd give you a ride tonight. She's got her license now, you know."

And so it was all smoothed over and settled. Or so I thought. I was really looking forward to playing tonight and having some friends there to pad out the audience. Anyway, I went straight home from school and tore through my closet, which is really pretty sparse. And although I don't consider myself a particularly fashion-conscious or vain person, I don't know how many times I changed my clothes this afternoon, trying to figure out what looked the best. And then finally I just settled on an old black T-shirt with my ripped denim vest, blue jeans, and my purple Doc Martens. I know, pretty boring, but it was getting late and my dad was ready to go.

"Are you going to stay and watch?" I asked as he pulled up to the front door of the cafe. It was pouring down rain, and I waited in the car for his response. But to be honest, I wasn't sure whether I really wanted him there or not.

"Didn't Mom mention that we're going to a Halloween party at the Stephensens tonight?"

I could tell he felt sort of bad. "Oh, that's okay, Dad." I grabbed up my guitar case. "It's not like it's any big deal."

"When do you need to be picked up?"

"I can get a ride home from Laura." Although I hadn't checked with her to be sure, I thought she probably wouldn't mind.

He smiled. "Okay, honey, then break a leg."

I laughed. "Yeah, sure." Then I ducked out into the rain and sprinted for the door.

I'd purposely arrived about twenty minutes early, hoping to sort of settle in and get comfortable. But it was anything but comforting to find that the place was almost completely deserted. The only customer was a tired-looking mom with two preschoolers dressed up like a dragon and a pumpkin. And they just chased each other around the tables and squealed a lot while she quickly gulped down a cup of cappuccino.

"Hi, Mike," I said as I set my guitar case next to the small stage, which was now cleared of chairs and looked strangely empty and slightly intimidating with its solitary stool and lone microphone.

"Wanna coffee?" he asked. "On the house."

"Sure. I'll have a mocha."

I sat on a stool next to the counter and took a deep cleansing breath—to help me relax a little. It's something my mom taught me to do as a little kid. "So, do you expect anyone to show up tonight?" I asked when he finally set the cup down in front of me.

"Don't know. It's kinda sporadic around here. Some nights I'm about ready to shut the place down and suddenly it starts popping. Then other nights when I really expect a crowd, it'll be deader than a doornail." He grinned as he wiped down the counter. "Now, just how dead is a doornail anyway?"

I shrugged. "Guess it's not a real live wire."

He glanced toward the window. "Then we get this crummy weather tonight, plus it's Halloween..." He shook his head. "Maybe it was a mistake on my part to schedule you at all."

"Oh, it's okay." I took a sip of my coffee and tried not to show my real disappointment. "I can just play around and think of it as a practice night."

He nodded. "Yeah, it helps to be laid-back around here."

Then the mom and her two kids left, and it was only Mike and me. "Well, I invited a couple friends to come by." I smiled lamely.

"Every little bit helps."

At eight o'clock, I stepped onto the stage and sat on the tall stool and started just quietly picking around on my guitar. A man and a woman had come in a few minutes earlier and were now seated over by the wall, as far from the stage as possible. Their heads were bent toward each other as they talked in hushed tones, as if they didn't want to be disturbed. It was painfully clear they hadn't come to see me. So for a few hour-long minutes, I pretended I was only there to play background music, and I tried to keep it low and calm.

And really it wasn't so bad. Okay, a little humiliating, I suppose, but then I hadn't come here for some big ego trip either. Or so I kept telling myself. After about twenty minutes, a few more people drifted in, including Laura and several of her friends as well as Allie. And at around eight-thirty Cesar, Jake, and Spencer came in along with a couple of guys I don't know too well. So the crowd was gradually increasing, and I decided it was time to actually play some real songs.

"Hi, everyone," I said into the mike, interrupting some chatter. "My name is Chloe, and I'm glad you decided to come out tonight, especially in this lousy weather. But then I guess the rain probably put a damper on your trick-or-treating anyway." This brought a few snickers from some of the older crowd, but my friends kind of looked like they thought I was losing it. Then I started to play. At first it didn't seem as though they were really paying much attention to me. Some people were ordering coffees and snitching candy from Mike's trick or treat pumpkin, and others were just visiting.

But by the time I ended the first song, it was getting quieter. And before long, it felt as if they were really there to hear me play. Even the secluded couple off to the side had stopped talking and were both looking my way. I got a little nervous then. And I wondered what everyone was thinking. Like were they just being nice because I was playing so badly that they felt sorry for me? I purposely didn't allow much time to pause between songs, probably because I was so nervous and was afraid they might not clap. But usually they applauded then quieted down as I started again. Finally, after about six songs, I spoke into the mike again.

"So, how's it going out there?" And a few people (like my friends) tossed back some corny responses and I laughed.

"Okay, it's not like I'm fishing for compliments," I said. "But this is my first time actually performing at the Paradiso. So what do you think? Am I doing okay, or are you wishing you'd brought along some rotten tomatoes?"

Fortunately, their responses seemed fairly positive, so I continued for a few more songs until Mike came over and suggested I take a break. Now I wasn't sure whether to be relieved or worried then. Did he think I was messing up and wanted to shut me down? I knew I'd made a few mistakes on some of my songs, but I hoped no one had noticed but me.

"Here, Chloe, have a glass of water," he said. "You don't want to overdo it, you know."

I sipped the water. "But am I doing okay?" I asked as I set the glass down.

He grinned. "Sure, you're great. You're a natural."

"Really?" I stared at him with a mixture of wonder and relief. "You think so?"

"Just relax and enjoy it."

So I went over and sat at the table with my friends. And to my relief, they all started saying how great I was doing. Oh, sure, they threw in a few good-natured jabs and sarcastic jokes, but mostly they seemed to really like it. Except for Allie, that is. She didn't say anything. She kept fiddling with the handle on her coffee mug as if it was the most interesting thing in the whole room. And I could tell she was mad at me again. But I just didn't see why. And frankly, it irritated me that she was acting that way. I mean, if the roles were reversed, I think I'd be happy and excited for her. At least I would hope to be. Anyway, I decided to just ignore her. Why should I allow her selfish moodiness and jealousy to spoil my evening?

I went back up there and played for almost an hour, and the crowd actually started to grow as more people came in. And I don't think it was my imagination that they seemed to warm up to me even more as the evening progressed. I have to say, it was one of the coolest moments of my entire life. It was like something just clicked inside of me. Like I knew without a doubt that this was what I was meant for. Maybe it was a God-thing.

I played a varied selection of my songs, starting from my early ones that are full of questions and problems and, I'll admit, complain a lot about love and life and loss, and all sorts of things. Then I moved into my more recent songs—the ones that involve searching and then finding God. Oh,

I'm sure that most of the crowd didn't even know exactly what the words meant because my lyrics can sound a little confusing sometimes. But then that's okay. Hopefully, it gave them something to think about—if they wanted to, that is.

Just as I was starting to wrap up, I noticed that Allie was gone. I figured she was probably in the bathroom or something, but when I finally quit and joined Laura and the others, no one knew where she'd gone.

"I was just in the bathroom," said LaDonna. "And she's not there."

"Yeah, I thought she was going to ride home with me," said Laura. "But she must've changed her mind."

"Well, she didn't seem too happy tonight," I said as I pulled on my coat.

Just then I felt someone patting me on the back and turned to see Mike smiling at me. "That was great tonight, Chloe." He handed me an envelope. "Don't walk off without your check."

"Thanks." I pocketed the envelope. I'd actually forgotten that this was a paying gig. I know I would've happily done it for free. Of course, I won't tell Mike that.

"And let's get you in here again, okay?"

"Sure."

"I'll ask Jill, that's my wife, to give you a call and set it up—maybe on a regular basis."

I smiled. "Cool!"

"You ready?" asked Laura. "I promised to be home before ten."

"Yeah." I looked around the room again, still wondering about Allie. Then we went outside and dashed through the rain over to Laura's mom's car. "I sure hope Allie didn't walk home in this," I said once we were inside.

"Might chill her down," Laura said as she started the engine. The other girls laughed.

"What's the deal with her anyway?" asked Mercedes. "She's always moping around or acting like she's some big rock-and-roll diva. What's her big problem?"

"It's that Wicca thing," said LaDonna. "How can you be happy if you think you're a witch?"

They all laughed again.

"She's just confused," I offered in her defense. I was still feeling a little aggravated at her myself.

"Yeah, she's confused," said Laura. "She's got the devil leading her around by the nose. Sheesh, that would confuse anyone."

"Maybe she had to hurry off to some witches' convention tonight," said LaDonna. "After all, it is Halloween. Isn't that the big witch holiday of the year? Don't they have some weird deal where they get all dressed up and chant strange things in a circle or something?"

"I heard that some groups actually sacrifice animals and then drink their blood."

"Gross!" LaDonna shrieked. "You're making that up."

"No, I'm serious," said Mercedes. "I saw it on TV. And I've even heard that some groups sacrifice babies and homeless people and stuff."

"You guys know Allie's not into that kind of stuff," I said loudly, hoping to shut them down. "She says their main rule is not to hurt anyone—"

"Maybe they just kill them painlessly," suggested Mercedes in a spooky voice. "Just close your eyes, little girl, this won't hurt a bit."

"Oh, lighten up, you guys!" Laura pulled into my driveway. "Sorry about that, Chloe. They get a little carried away sometimes."

LaDonna laughed. "Hey, it's Halloween. We're supposed to get carried away. Can we go trick-or-treating at Andre's house now?"

"Thanks for the ride." I said as I sprang from the car and dashed toward the house. My parents weren't back yet so I poked around the refrigerator and then finally decided to call Allie to make sure she'd made it home okay. Of course, I figured I'd just get the usual busy signal. But to my surprise, her mom picked up. Now, I've only met Elise a couple of times, and although she seems a little high-strung and uptight, she's actually pretty nice.

"Hi, is Allie there?"

"No. Is this Chloe?" Her voice had that sharp edge again.

"Yeah."

"I thought Allie was with you at the coffee-house tonight."

"Well, she _was_ there..." I wasn't sure what to say now. I really didn't want to worry her.

"But she's not there now?"

"No, I'm home now. She rode over with Laura, but when it was time to leave, she was already gone. We thought maybe you'd picked her up or she walked home or something."

Elise groaned. "Oh, dear!"

"She'll probably be home any minute," I added, feeling guilty for bothering her or perhaps even getting Allie into trouble.

"Yeah, she better be. It's getting late."

So after I hung up I started getting worried too. Where could she be? I don't think Allie really knows that many people—besides the ones who were at the coffeehouse, that is. And I honestly don't think she has any real witch friends in our town. I think most of her connections are on-line. And even if she had walked home, she should've been there by now. So what's up? I'm really praying for her though. It feels to me as if she's in a dangerous place.

A PRECARIOUS PLACE

standing on the ledge and looking down
balanced on your tightrope like a clown
you don't know which way you want to turn
looking toward the darkness, feel the burn
don't you know you can't stay there forever?
it'll take you down to never-never
teetering back and forth will drive you mad
and everyone around you feels so sad
can't you see the hand that's reaching out?
don't you know that He has heard your shout?
can't you feel the love He has for you?
can't you see what's false and what is true?
don't you know your precipice is pride?
take His hand and walk along beside
the One who wants to lead you to the light
where the Son shine burns away the night
come on down from there, come with me
and meet the One whose love will set you free
take His hand and you will see it's true
His love is real and strong enough for you
amen

cm

Twelve

Tuesday, November 5

Life's been a busy blur these past few days, and I've been unable to write. So I'll try to bring my diary up-to-date now. Lots has been going on, but it seems minor compared to what's happened with Allie. Okay, I know this is confusing. I'd better start where I last left off.

I don't think I slept more than two hours straight on Halloween night. I'd gotten more and more worried about Allie. And then I kept having these terrifying thoughts that led to some really bizarre and frightening dreams. Then I'd wake up and pray for her. By the next day, I was so tired and worried that I felt like I was moving through the twilight zone. I tried to call Allie before I went to school, but no one answered. And then she wasn't anywhere to be seen at school. After choir I told Laura how freaked I was feeling.

"I know," she said. "I'm really worried too. I got to thinking about everything last night and, let me tell you, I was really doing some frantic praying for that girl."

"Yeah, me too. I just tried calling her house

again, and no one's home."

"Where could she be?"

"I don't know. I was even thinking of calling her mom at work, but I probably shouldn't."

Laura seemed to consider this. "Maybe not. I suppose there could be a perfectly logical explanation for everything."

Just then I saw Allie walking toward us. Man, I almost fell out of my chair as I leaped up to meet her.

"What happened to you?" I asked as I grabbed her. I didn't even care how stupid I looked or sounded. "We've been totally freaked. Where did you go? Why weren't you home?"

She just smiled.

"Allie?" I stared at her.

By then Laura had joined us. "What's going on with you, Al?" she demanded. "What do you mean by running off like that last night. Don't you know we were—?"

"Sorry." Allie held up both hands. "Give me a break, will you? If you two could just chill for a minute, I might even explain." She looked from Laura to me. "That is, if you really want to hear it."

"Of course, we want to hear everything." I led her to an empty table and the three of us sat down. "What is going on?"

Allie smiled again. And suddenly I thought,

okay, she's flipping out on us. She's probably gone off and joined some coven or occult thing, and we're losing her completely now. Because honestly, I'd never seen such a goofy expression on her face. "Come on," I urged her. "Can't you see we're dying here?"

"Okay." She nodded. "Well, I was pretty bummed last night."

"Because of me?" I asked.

"I thought that was it, but it wasn't. It was because of me. Anyway, I got fed up and just took off and went outside for a smoke. Then once I was outside, I started walking."

"In the rain?" asked Laura.

"Yeah, I was soaked within minutes. But I didn't really notice it. I just kept walking. I didn't even know where I was going. But it's like something was pulling me—like a physical force, you know?"

I nodded.

"But it wasn't a good force. It's like it was pulling me toward something that was evil and dark—something that felt totally hopeless and destructive."

Laura nodded now. "Yeah, that's what I thought."

Allie eyed her curiously. "What do you mean?"

"When I was praying for you—"

"You were praying for me?"

"Yeah, I was really concerned."

"Me too," I chimed in. "I was so freaked I could hardly sleep at all last night." I pointed to my eyes. "See these dark shadows? They have your name written all over them."

"I'm sorry." She looked at both of us and actually seemed sorry. "Anyway, I remembered your story about going to the cemetery—"

"You went up to the cemetery?" I looked at her like she was crazy. "In the middle of the night—on Halloween?"

She nodded. "And I have to admit it was pretty scary, and I wondered what on earth I was doing up there. I mean, it's like I almost don't remember walking up there."

"And?" demanded Laura. "What happened?"

"Well, I just walked around, and before long I was crying—actually sobbing, really. It's like I was sadder than I've ever been before. I felt like giving up, like I really wanted to die. As if life was too hard and too disappointing and it was never going to get any better for me." She looked down at her hands. "I know it sounds really melodramatic, but it's the truth. I just wanted to end the pain."

Laura reached over and put her hand on Allie's arm. I wanted to do the exact same thing but thought it might look phony. "Then what happened?" I asked quietly.

"Well, it's kind of embarrassing." She looked

up at us again. "But I'll tell you two—since you were praying for me. I actually laid down right on top of a grave—"

"You're kidding?" Laura's eyes grew wide. "You actually laid on a grave on Halloween night?"

Allie nodded. "I know it sounds totally bizarre. I don't even know why I did it. It was stupid and weird and—" She slowly shook her head. "But it's like I just wanted to die and be buried and over with. And I somehow thought that lying on the grave might actually kill me."

Laura sighed. "Yeah, I think I would've died of fright."

"How long did you lay there?"

She shrugged. "I don't really know. It's kind of like I went into a daze or fell asleep or something. But I came to and then I got really, really scared. I mean, like heart-about-to-burst scared. I've never been so terrified in my life. It's like something evil was right there with me. I could feel it."

I reached over and grabbed her arm. "What did you do?"

"I got up and just ran for my life."

"Your apartment's a long ways from there," I said.

"Yeah. I was crying and running and thinking I was for sure going to keel over with a heart attack and die, and then I got to the street that

your church is on. And even though my house isn't
far away from there, it felt like miles. But there
were lights on in the parking lot, and I saw
Willy's old car there. He was getting into it, and I
just ran over there and literally started pounding on the hood of his car."

"You're kidding?" I stared at her in wonder.

"Yeah, I really freaked the poor guy out. He
didn't recognize me at first because I was such a
mess. He told me later that he thought I was some
kid tripping out on some bad acid or something."
She turned and looked at me. "Did you know that
Willy had a history with LSD?"

I shook my head.

"Yeah, anyway, he let me into his car even
though I was all muddy and gross and wet and
then he asked me what was wrong."

"What did you tell him?" asked Laura.

"I said I thought I was losing my mind. I told
him what I'd done and then asked if he thought I
was going crazy. He just laughed and said, 'No way,
I think you're going sane.' And then he said he
thought that God was trying to get through to me,
but that the devil was trying to mess things up.
Then he told me about what happened to him back
in the seventies after he'd gotten back from
Vietnam. He had that thing the soldiers get where
they have those horrible flashbacks to the war."

"Post-traumatic stress syndrome?" I suggested.

"Something like that. Anyway, he started traveling with that rock band and experimenting with drugs, and it finally really messed up his head. He had an episode kinda like mine, only I'm guessing lots worse, where he thought he was going crazy too. But during that time he kept running into this guy named Brian who was a Christian, and Brian kept telling him how much God loved him. And finally, Willy said he just gave in to God and says that his life's been on track ever since. He quit taking drugs cold turkey, and even though he still has flashbacks from the war occasionally, he prays his way through them and always asks God to teach him something through it."

"Cool." I squeezed Allie's arm. "And?"

She smiled. "And... so, I did it too."

"You invited Jesus into your heart?" Laura leaned over and peered into her face.

Allie nodded. "Yep, I did."

Then, just as the warning bell rang, we all three jumped up and laughed and actually hugged and made total fools of ourselves as everyone else started heading back to class.

And so I'm thinking, doesn't God have a great sense of humor? That He would save Allie on Halloween night. Isn't that the greatest?

The next day we three jammed like we've never jammed before. And suddenly I'm thinking, hey, why couldn't we be a band? Maybe that's exactly why God brought us together in the first place; maybe that's what He had planned all along. Still, I'm not saying this out loud to anyone yet. I'm just praying that God will show us what's right and lead us where we need to go. And I'm already booked at the Paradiso again during the week before Thanksgiving. I haven't told Allie yet. Not that she'd react badly. But right now it's cool just focusing on what's happening with her life. And I'm trying to be a good friend.

ALLIE'S SONG
she took the leap
from death to life
she took the step
amid the strife
she grabbed onto
a faith that heals
and she escaped
the one who kills
her face is like
a lamp that's bright
her eyes are full
of love and light
she threw away
her witch's charms
and ran into
her Father's arms

thank you, God!
amen
cm

Tuesday, November 19

I know, I know; I've been very negligent of my diary lately. But it's only because so much is happening right now. I've been baby-sitting for Tony and Steph, jamming with Laura and Allie, practicing after school with our small ensemble group, and then going to church it seems every time the doors are opened (Allie cannot seem to get enough of it!). Whew!

And tonight I played again at the Paradiso Café. To a nice-sized crowd too. Even my parents and the Stephensens came. And to my surprise I was much more relaxed and at ease than the last time. Oh, I still got the butterflies in the stomach thing, but once I got going and just focused on my music, it went away. It was actually quite fun. And my parents and their friends seemed fairly impressed. Mr. Stephensen teaches music at the local college, and he thinks I'm pretty good. He told my dad I should consider recording a CD. And who knows, maybe I will. It would've been a perfect evening except for one thing.

"You know, you sounded really great up there, Chloe," my mom said. But there was this little catch in her voice. I could tell she wanted to say something else too.

"Thanks." I leaned into the backseat and prepared myself.

"But maybe you should think about how you look up there too."

Okay, there it was. "What do you mean, Mom?" I tried not to let defensiveness creep into my voice. This is a battle I've been trying to avoid since giving my heart to God.

"Oh, you know. Maybe you should think of doing something different with your hair—or maybe we could go shopping for some new clothes."

"Mom, I like the way I look."

The car got silent then.

"She looks like a performer," my dad said as he pulled into the garage.

"I suppose." But I could tell my mom wasn't convinced. And this really bugged me.

Once we were inside, I set down my guitar and turned to my mom. "I don't see why you can't just accept me for who I am, Mom." I held out my arms. "This is how I wanna look. This is Chloe Miller. No, it's not Joy Miller, head cheerleader extraordinaire. But it's who I am. And as far as I can see, it's not going to change."

She frowned. "But you look like a punk rocker, and your music isn't like that."

"You only heard one part of my music tonight.

You should listen in when Allie and Laura and I are jamming. It can get pretty wild up there."

My dad laughed. "Yeah, the walls are usually thumping down here."

"But maybe more people would be drawn to your music," continued my mom, "if you looked more, oh, you know, mainstream."

Well, fortunately that made me laugh. "Yeah, sure, it might draw more old people like you and Dad, but that's not really who I'm aiming for."

"Hey, who you calling old?" Dad pretended to be offended. "I grew up listening to the same kind of music that you're imitating."

I patted him on the back. "No offense, Dad, but you guys are my parents. You're supposed to be a little out of the loop. That's how we play the game, right?"

Still, I could tell my mom wasn't convinced. In fact, I'm pretty certain she was mad as she turned around and acted as though she was absorbed with putting a couple of glasses into the dishwasher. So I just left and went to my room. I don't know how to get through to her. To be honest, I don't even understand her. She seems to be all about pretense and show and superficiality. And as much as I hate to admit it, those are traits I despise. And that makes me feel horribly guilty because she is my mother. But I don't get why she's like that. Why are appearances so important to her? More important

than people... I think. What's really disturbing is
to think she's like so many of the shallow people
(like Tiffany Knight) that I have such a hard time
loving at school. Oh, God, help me!

WHO'S RIGHT AND WHO'S WRONG?
what if it's me?
what if i am the hypocrite here?
pretending to love everyone equally
yet hating the ones who just don't get it
the ones who are so pathetically insecure
that they appear shallow, uncaring,
judgmental, and cruel
but don't they need to be loved too?
and yet i cannot love them
when i can barely tolerate them
how many times must i bite my tongue
acting like it's okay
i'm okay, you're okay, everyone's okay
when in reality i cannot stand them
i am a hypocrite
a pretense of love yet
full of ugliness and hatred
God, forgive me
make me more like You
and less like me
help me to love the way You do
amen
cm

Thirteen

Monday, November 25

I am really trying to act more mature—more like Jesus. Less judgmental and more loving. But it's not always easy. Like yesterday.

Maybe it was a guilt trip, but somehow my mom talked me into going shopping with her after church—at the mall even. I really didn't want to go, but she was so insistent—and hopeful. And as I said, I'm trying, really trying, not to be judgmental.

"You know it's impossible for me to pick out anything that you'd like," she explained. "So you've got to come along and help me."

Why are we doing this? I kept screaming inside my head. But like a trained poodle I patiently trotted along beside her as we trekked from store to store. Fortunately, I did manage to find a couple of things that I actually liked and, well, that she probably barely tolerated. But she acted as if it was all fine and good until we were driving home. Then she dropped one of her little bombshells. That's how I think of them. Like she says this little thing that could easily be harmless, but it just seems to blow up like dynamite inside of me. Still, I hoped we could defuse this one before it was too late.

"I had always hoped that my daughter would like clothes and shopping," she said as we left the crowded parking lot.

"Oh, Mom," I began, feeling like here we go again. "You know, I'm just not like that."

"I know. But it could be so fun. Karen at work is always telling me how she and her daughter have such fun shopping and sharing clothes. And, well..."

"You wish I were like that." I turned and looked out the window.

"After raising two boys, you think your daughter will be different."

I laughed. "I am different, Mom."

She frowned. "You know what I mean."

So I thought about it for a while. I've been asking God to help me in this specific area with my mom, and suddenly I wondered if I was about to lose some great opportunity. "I guess I just don't get it. I can't really see what's so great about shopping and clothes and looking a certain way." I turned and looked at her in her perfect designer outfit with coordinating jewelry. Even her shoes and purse go together. "Why is it so important to you?"

Now this seemed to throw her for a loop, and I

could tell she was trying to brush me off. "Oh, it's not that important, Chloe."

"But it is, Mom. You won't go anywhere unless you look absolutely perfect. Even Dad complains about it sometimes. And I'm not saying it's wrong. I mean, I think you look really nice and everything, but it's just not for me. Still, I have to wonder sometimes, why are you like that? Do you even know?"

She thought about it. "I'm not sure, Chloe. I suspect it has to do with how I was raised."

"But Grandma's not like that. In fact, she seems pretty normal to me."

She laughed. "Well, she would to you." She hit her hand on the steering wheel. "Maybe that's it!"

"What?"

"Maybe I was trying really hard not to be like my mother, and now you're trying hard not to be like me."

I considered this. "I don't think I'm trying not to be like you, Mom. I think I'm just trying to be me."

"Well, that's how I felt too."

"So, what was Grandma like when you were growing up? What was so bad that you wanted to be different?" All I could think of Grandma Brown was how she loves to cook and sew and garden and how I always feel warm and welcome in her old-fashioned farmhouse. She remarried

when I was about five and now lives a couple
hours away from us.

"You know my parents got divorced when I was
little. And my mom just barely scraped by." Mom
made a face. "It used to embarrass me almost to
death in grade school to see my mom wearing a
hair net and working in the cafeteria. If she was
up front serving the food, I would duck my head
down and just look at my tray as I passed by. I
never even said hi."

I nodded. "Yeah, I suppose I can understand
that. I probably would've felt the same way if you
were working in the cafeteria."

She glanced at me. "You would?"

"Yeah. It's always kinda embarrassing having
your parents around no matter how cool they are,
or aren't."

"I guess so. But my mother was definitely <u>not</u>
cool. She wore these horrible housedresses
everywhere she went. Do you know what a housedress is, Chloe?"

"Not really." Grandma usually just wears
jeans and sweatshirts and casual stuff now.

"Well, a housedress is this frumpy thing in
awful colors with snaps that go down the front."
She groaned. "<u>Very ugly.</u>"

"Maybe it was all she could afford."

She nodded. "You're probably right. And I have
to give her credit because she did manage to

scrape together enough money to buy fabric and sew nice-looking clothes for me."

"She's a good seamstress."

"But just the same, I was always ashamed of her. And as soon as I was old enough to work—baby-sitting, housecleaning, whatever—I started buying and even making my own clothes. And I suppose it became very important to me to look a certain way."

I was starting to get it now. "So you could rise above it all?"

"Yeah. That's probably what I was trying to do. I didn't like being poor or having a single mom who always looked frumpy. I think I was trying to make up for it with my own appearance—so kids wouldn't make fun of me."

We were at a stoplight now, and she turned and looked at me and I think I saw tears in her eyes.

"But do you love Grandma?" I asked.

"Of course, I do." She turned and looked straight ahead. "But I don't completely understand her. She has more money now that she's married to Fred, and she could afford to dress better if she wanted. And sometimes I'll get her something pretty for her birthday or Christmas and she'll just put it away in her closet. I don't understand that."

I thought maybe I did but knew I would never be able to explain it to my mom.

"And I know that she's like you, Chloe. She often tells me that I worry too much about appearances. And maybe she's right. Maybe you both are. I don't know. But the truth is, I _like_ pretty things. I _like_ shopping and I _like_ feeling as if I look attractive." She glanced at me again. "Is there anything terribly wrong with that?"

"I don't think so, Mom. Maybe the thing that bugs me is that sometimes it feels like you're trying to push those things on me. I mean, how would you feel if Grandma and I tried to get you to dress like us?"

She laughed. "That'd be pretty funny."

"Right. So maybe if you think about how you'd feel if the roles were reversed, well, maybe it would help you to understand us better."

"Chloe, you're pretty smart for a kid."

I laughed now. "Gee, thanks."

"No, really. I wasn't nearly as mature as you are back when I was fifteen. I was completely obsessed with clothes and boys and popularity. But you're different. It's as if you were born old."

"Yeah, that's what Grandma says too."

"I think I'll give her a call when we get home."

I smiled. "Tell her hi for me."

Oh, it's obvious that Mom and I will probably never be best friends, not like those mothers and daughters who share clothes and giggle about boys. But maybe today was a step of progress. I

think I understand her a little more, but to be
honest, I really relate better to Grandma.

WHY WE ARE THE WAY WE ARE
God, You are so very clever
innovative, creative, and forever
i am who i am it's plain to see
You tossed away the mold when You made me
and yet i know You know just what You're doing
and there shall be no crying or boo-hooing
for i believe i'm real and not a fake
and i believe that You make no mistake
amen
cm

Monday, December 2

Allie, Laura, and I are now practicing several
songs to do for the church's Christmas concert. It
was Willy's idea. One is a rearrangement of an old
Christmas carol and the other two are my own
creations. And one of them I'll do solo (both Allie
and Laura are okay with this) because it just
seems to work best for the song. But it's fun practicing together—especially now that we're all on
the same spiritual page! And Willy talked us into
practicing at the church so that Allie can have a
decent drum set to play on, plus the acoustics are
better.

I'm also playing a couple evenings at the Paradiso (and Mike has promised to have our whole little group there after the New Year—yippee!). Plus I'm singing a couple of solos in our school Christmas concert. So December is quite the performing month for me! I feel, well, almost famous! Ha-ha!

So I should be flying high now, right? Wrong. Unfortunately, I have this old thing still doggin' at my heels. And it seems to bring out the very worst in me. It's like as soon as I think I'm doing pretty good as a Christian, this thing comes up again. I suppose it's not nice to call her a "thing" since she's really a human. At least I think she is. Sometimes I wonder though. Yes, it's Tiffany Knight. And for some reason she just seems to have it out for me. It's like every day is open season on Chloe Miller. And today, I'm afraid I just blew it.

I think things started getting worse after my second time playing at the Paradiso Café. You see, this small ensemble group that I'm in also has a couple of very popular girls in it—girls that Tiffany would kill to be friends with. And to be honest, these girls really aren't half bad. One's name is Cortney Stein and the other is Torrey Barnes. Anyway, I guess one of them overheard me talking to Mr. Thompson about my little coffee-house gig the previous week.

"Hey, Chloe," she said to me just before choir today. "Is it true that you actually performed at the Paradiso Café?"

I smiled. "Yeah. It was my second time there."

"That is so rad." She reached over and tapped me on the arm with her finger. "It's like you're famous now. Can I touch you?"

I laughed. "Yeah, playing at the coffeehouse, my only claim to fame."

"Hey, it's a start."

And I have to admit it was kinda cool hearing her approval. I'm not even sure why. And, okay, I may never be her best friend, and I sure wouldn't be willing to conform myself to the way she and her friends look and act, but it was sort of fun just the same. But here's the downside.

Unfortunately, Tiffany witnessed this little exchange. And after choir today, after I picked up a new arrangement for one of the Christmas songs from Mr. Thompson, she came up to me in the hall and said, "Hey, Spike, can I touch you too?" in her snooty voice and then punched me in the arm, hard.

"Hey!" I rubbed my arm. "What's your problem?"

She just laughed. "I wanted to touch the famous singer. Is anything wrong with that?" I glanced around to see if I could spy Laura down the hall, but she was nowhere in sight. In fact, the hallway looked pretty deserted.

Then her friend Kerry did the same thing, only her punch felt even harder. And then, for no explainable reason, other than I'm still human and I still blow it sometimes, I reacted. I reacted badly. Okay, I'm sure some people would say it was understandable and maybe even self-defense. But I still know it was wrong.

I hadn't put my backpack over my shoulder yet, and so after Kerry's punch, I just gave my pack a good swing and let it fly, whacking Kerry (the closest one to me) right smack in the face. As soon as I heard it hit her face, I knew it was a mistake. A great big, stupid mistake. I probably had more than twenty pounds of books in there. And when my pack came down, her nose was bleeding.

"I—I'm—" But before I could finish my sentence Tiffany was screaming, crying for help, and yelling like I was trying to kill her poor friend.

By then Mr. Thompson came out to see what was going on. "What happened?" he demanded when he saw Tiffany. But then he saw the blood coming from Kerry's nose and put his arm around her and quickly escorted her to the office with Tiffany right on his heels.

I know I should've followed, but somehow I couldn't. I was too angry and embarrassed and sorry and mad and just plain confused to even think straight. And I didn't go to the cafeteria either. I just went outside and walked around in the cold, begging God to forgive me and to help me out of this humiliating little scrape. I almost didn't even go to fifth period but didn't want to get into trouble for skipping as well. It was about midway through geometry when the office aide came in and handed a note to Mr. Henderson.

"Chloe Miller?" he said in his normally stern voice.

I went up and he told me they wanted to see me in the counselor's office. Well, everyone knows when you're summoned to "the counselor's office" that something is wrong—that you're in trouble. And looking very much, I'm sure, like the old Chloe Miller, the one who didn't mind trouble, I held up my head and walked out of that room. But I didn't feel like the old Chloe Miller. Today I felt upset and sad and a little scared. I wasn't even sure why. I prayed as I walked toward Mrs. King's office.

"Have a seat," she said.

I sat and waited, looking at her neatly arranged desk. She seemed neatly arranged too, with perfectly styled hair and a silk scarf around her neck.

"Do you know why you're here, Chloe?"

I nodded. "I hit Kerry in the face with my backpack."

"Right." She glanced out the window. "Did you know that Kerry's nose appears to be broken?"

"No." I stared at Mrs. King in horror. "It's really broken?"

She nodded. "And did you know that Kerry can press assault charges and the police can be involved?"

I swallowed hard. I felt like I was about to cry, and maybe it was the old tough me, or just my foolish pride, but I didn't want to cry right there in Mrs. King's office. I looked down at my lap in silence.

"Chloe?"

I looked up.

"Tiffany has already made a statement. Now, I need to get yours. What exactly happened today?"

So, fighting to hold back the tears, I told her. But I didn't just tell her about today, I also told her about the day when Tiffany and her thugs beat me up and about other days when they'd teased me in the past.

"Were there any witnesses?"

"Not today. But Laura Mitchell has been around before. And other girls too. Tiffany and her friends pick on a lot of girls that are—" I choked now and I could feel a tear slipping out—"different."

"I see."

But I looked up at her and wondered: Do you really see? Sitting behind the protection of your tidy desk with your neat designer suit and expensive jewelry do you really see what it's like for the rest of us, for the ones who don't fit in?

"This stuff happens all the time," I told her. "Some people simply cannot accept that other people are different. Then if someone different actually starts to succeed at something, well, that really makes her mad. Do you understand what I'm saying here?" I'm afraid I probably sounded a little desperate—like I was ranting or something, but I really wanted to make my point. Then, to my surprise, she actually smiled.

"I probably understand better than you think." She pushed a gold bracelet up on her wrist. "I know how it feels to be different."

"Really?"

"Yes. Despite how you perceive me, I've experienced the same thing myself. And, what's worse, I see what kids do to each other—every single day."

"And you can't do anything about it?"

"I'm trying, but believe me it's an uphill battle."

"So, what should I do then? I mean, about Kerry pressing charges and everything?"

She shrugged. "I don't really know, besides waiting, that is. Although, I do think an apology is in order."

I looked down at my lap. Just then I was thinking, it doesn't seem fair, Kerry and Tiffany attacked me first; I only reacted.

"But you'll have to decide what's best for you," she said as she set down her pen. "And even if you apologize, Kerry may still choose to press charges. Do you think Laura Mitchell would be willing to make a statement about how these girls have harassed you in the past?"

"She might. You could ask her."

"Okay, then. Anyone else?"

So I told her a couple more names, including Allie, who's been the target of some of their snipes in the past. "Do you really think this will help?" I asked as I stood up. "I mean, I hate getting all these guys involved if it's only going to turn into a big mess. The reason I never told anyone about getting beat up before was because I figured it wouldn't solve anything—I thought it would only make Tiffany go after me harder. And back then I didn't even have any friends to back me up."

"I'm afraid a lot of kids feel that way. A bunch of stuff goes unreported around here. And then even when something is reported, you can never tell which way it will go. It's usually just one person's word against another's. Unless there's a reliable witness. Still, if anything is going to change, people have to come forward and tell the truth."

"Thanks for listening, Mrs. King."

She nodded. "I hope this turns out okay."

"Yeah, me too."

So tonight I told my parents about the whole thing. And instead of getting upset, which for some reason I'd expected (probably due to some of the scrapes I'd gotten into during the past year), they were surprisingly supportive.

"I wish you'd told us about all this when that awful girl beat you up the first time," my mom said as she started clearing the table.

"Yeah," my dad agreed, "then we could be witnesses for you. Did you tell anyone about it when it happened?"

I shook my head. "I was kinda embarrassed, and I didn't really have any close friends at the time. In fact, the only way I had to vent was to write about it in my diary—"

"That's it!" My dad almost dropped a plate. "Your diary! That could be used as evidence in a court of law."

"My diary in a courtroom? But I don't want anyone reading my personal—"

"They wouldn't need to read all of it. Just that particular—"

"Oh, honey," my mom interrupted. "Surely, it won't go that far."

But I'm not so sure anymore. Tonight I decided to write a letter of apology to Kerry. Because, despite the fact that she and Tiffany started the whole thing, I am sorry that I didn't control myself, and that her nose got broken. If I could do today all over again, I would definitely not sling my backpack at her.

So I tried to put all these thoughts, as well as many others, into what I hoped was a sincere and sensible letter. And then, probably as a result of all this legal mumbo-jumbo, I slipped down to my dad's office and made a copy of my letter to keep on hand. Who knows why? But I'm tucking it into my diary just to be safe. Tomorrow, I plan to give Kerry my letter, as well as say I'm sorry in person—face-to-face. I don't expect it to be easy, but I believe that's what God wants me to do.

I'M SORRY

there is so much i'm sorry for
hatred, lies, greed, and war
i'm sorry that I'm not perfect
or that i failed to reflect
before i let my temper flare
before i cast away all care
fueled by hate i let You down
i forgot You were around
and that You had a better way
oh, dear God, what can i say?
i'm sorry
so sorry
cm

Fourteen

Tuesday, December 3

As I walked down the halls today, I felt like a convicted felon. It seemed as though everyone at school was staring at me or whispering behind my back. As if they all knew that I'd broken Kerry's nose.

It was some consolation that I had the support of my friends.

"I wish I'd waited for you yesterday," said Laura. "We should know better than to leave anyone isolated when Tiffany's on the prowl."

"But why was she on the prowl?" I asked.

"Didn't you hear?" said Laura. "LaDonna said that she overhead Tiffany make a mean remark about you to Torrey Barnes in choir yesterday, and Torrey told her to shut up."

"Man, I wish I'd known about that yesterday."

"Why didn't you tell me about this whole thing?" demanded Allie. "You should've at least called and told me what happened. I only found out about it this morning when I saw Laura. She said you called her last night."

"Actually, Allie, I tried to call you, but your line was busy."

She patted me on the back. "Sorry 'bout that. My mom was talking to her sister last night."

"What happens now?" asked Laura.

"I'm not sure. Mrs. King said we'd just have to wait and see what happens, like whether or not Kerry presses assault charges."

"You gotta be kidding?" Allie shook her head. "But those two started it."

"I know, but it's my word against theirs. And there are two of them."

"But everyone knows they're liars and bullies," said Laura.

"I don't know about that. They're pretty good at keeping up a good image when the right people are looking their way. Anyway, maybe it'll just blow over. I went ahead and wrote an apology to Kerry last night. Have you guys seen her anywhere?"

"Yeah, I saw her in first period," said Allie. "She's got this big, white bandage on her nose. And to be honest, I didn't feel a bit sorry for her. But now I feel sorta guilty about it. I mean, I know it's wrong to hate her."

"Yeah, I'm really praying about this whole thing and that God will help me to love her—and Tiffany too." I swallowed hard. "But it's not easy."

Allie shook her head. "Man, I'm glad it's you and not me. I know I would handle it all wrong."

I finally saw Kerry on my way to choir, but she

had a horde of girls around her, including Tiffany. I could tell by their expressions that there was no way I was going to get through to Kerry without risking either serious physical injury or perhaps more accusations. It might've just been me, but it felt as though even Mr. Thompson was looking at me with suspicion. It's as if everyone thought I was this horrible bully, so I left the minute choir was over and went straight to Mrs. King's office.

"I'm sorry to disturb you at lunchtime," I said.

"That's okay; come on in."

I handed her the letter. "I wrote this for Kerry, but she's got all her friends sticking really close, like they're protecting her or something. So I thought maybe you could give it to her for me."

She nodded. "I'm glad you stopped by. I was going to call you in here this afternoon."

"Why?" I felt my heart sink. Was Kerry pressing charges against me? Would the police come to school and pick me up, frisk and cuff me in front of everyone?

"Sit down, Chloe."

I sank into the chair and leaned over and put my head in my hands. Why was this happening to me? I'd been trying to do everything right, and it seemed as if things were really changing for me—with God, with friends, with music. And now this.

"I just don't get it. I don't know what to do."

"Kerry's parents were in this morning, and they plan to press charges."

I shook my head. "It figures."

"Does your family have a lawyer?"

I shrugged. "Yeah, I guess so."

"Do you want me to call them?"

"If you want. But it's okay; I can call them."

"You'll need to make a statement for the police. It'd probably be good if your lawyer was present."

Now I started to cry again. I mean, how could this be happening? Just because I reacted to being picked on? Because I'd slung my backpack? It all seemed so unjust. What was God doing about it anyway?

"Are you listening, Chloe?"

I nodded. "It's just, uh, pretty upsetting. It's so unfair."

"I know. There's a lot about life that's not fair."

"What am I supposed to do now? Do I go back to class? Will the police come and get me?"

"I suggest that you call your parents and your attorney and go directly to the police with your story. It will save you some embarrassment."

"Okay."

"Go ahead and use my phone if you like."

So I called my dad and told him what Mrs. King

had just said. I could tell he was irritated by the
edge in his voice, but I wasn't sure if it was about
the situation or just me. Then I waited in the
office for him to pick me up. I haven't felt so low
since before I asked God into my life. I reminded
myself about the roller-coaster metaphor. But
this felt worse than a bad dip. This felt like a
major derailment.

My dad was pretty quiet as we drove to the
police station. "Jim's going to meet us there," he
said as we got out of the car. "I told him about
your diary and he thinks that might help." Then
he cussed. And my dad's not the kind of guy who
normally does that. "This is just so stupid!"

"What?" I wondered if he was mad at me.

"That parents would press charges about
something that happened in school. It's like we
live in this lawsuit-crazy era. I don't know. But
it's moronic."

I nodded. At least he didn't seem to be mad at
me. Still, we wouldn't have been walking into the
police station if I had controlled my temper.

After a long wait, we went into a small room
with a policeman and Jim Collier, our lawyer.
They filled out some preliminary paperwork, and
then the officer asked me to tell him what happened. I told them everything I could remember,
including the time when Tiffany and Kerry had
beaten me up.

"But there were no witnesses that time either?" asked the officer.

I shook my head. "And I was too embarrassed to tell anyone."

"Embarrassed?" the officer looked confused.

"Well, I was trying to act like a tough girl then." I tried to smile, but I'm sure it looked pathetic.

"But she wrote about it in her diary," my dad offered hopefully. "That's evidence, isn't it?"

The officer looked back down at his paperwork. "Which arm did they punch yesterday?"

I rubbed my right arm. "This one."

"Are you willing to roll up your sleeve?" asked the officer.

"You don't have to," Jim said quickly.

I shrugged. "I don't really care. I doubt that there's anything to see anyway." So I rolled up my sleeve.

"Hey, there's definitely a bruise there," said Jim. "Can we get someone in here to photograph that?"

"Yeah, in a minute." The officer looked over his notes again. "And no one was around to witness the fight yesterday?"

"It wasn't really a fight," I said again. "And, no, I didn't see anyone. Not until Mr. Thompson came out."

"Apparently he didn't see anything, just heard yelling in the hallway."

I considered telling him about what LaDonna had overheard—when Tiffany dissed on me and Torrey Barnes told her to shut up. But I wasn't sure if he would understand the implication there, or maybe he'd just think I was being petty.

"I think that takes care of it, for now anyway." The officer gathered his paperwork and stood. "I'll send in someone to take a picture of that arm."

After he left I turned to Mr. Collier. "Are they going to put me in jail now?"

He smiled. "No, Chloe, I don't think so."

"This is so stupid!" My dad hit his fist on the table.

"I'm sorry, Dad."

He put his arm around me. "No, that's not what I mean, Pumpkin. It's not your fault."

"Yeah, it is. If I just hadn't swung my backpack..."

My dad turned to Mr. Collier. "Maybe we should press charges against Kerry and Tiffany for their attack on Chloe last fall."

"We might consider that."

I put my head down on the table and groaned. The idea of taking those girls to court made me feel sick. "Oh, Dad," I moaned. "I just want this to be over with. I want my life back."

My dad didn't want me go back to school afterward. That was a relief since I knew everyone would still be staring at me. It's possible that this whole thing would've blown over by now—if Kerry and her parents hadn't decided to press charges. As it is, Mr. Collier warned us that even the press would get involved now.

"As crazy as it sounds, this is just the kind of story they love—school violence—no one is safe. Sure, it's not as big as McFadden High School or someone carrying a firearm, but it's worth a blurb on the six o'clock news when nothing else is going on in town."

My dad warned me not to open the door or answer the phone. So I went to my room and replayed the whole thing over and over in mind—trying to figure out what I could've done or said differently (other than the obvious, like not slinging my backpack). But the more I thought about everything, the more confused I felt, and finally I just got down on my knees and prayed.

I WILL HANG ON TO YOU
oh, God, it feels like i'm in the pit of darkness
right now
are You here with me?
can You hear me?
will You help me?
You have been my very best friend, oh, God
please don't abandon me now
and i will hang on to You

even when it feels like i'm losing
i will hang on to You
even when everyone hates me
i will hang on to You
even when i want to give up
i will hang on to You
and i know You will hang on to me
when i am too weak
to hang on to You
please, don't let me slip away
amen
cm

Fifteen

Wednesday, December 4

My parents said I didn't have to go to school today, but for some reason I thought I should. To stay home seemed to admit my guilt. Not that I'm not guilty—I know what I did was wrong. But I also know that I'm not the only one at fault here. I just wish (and have been praying) that the whole truth could be brought to light.

During second period I was called into Mrs. King's office again. I walked through the deserted halls thinking, okay, here it comes. The police are probably down there right now, waiting to cuff me up and take me downtown. I know it was a stupid thought (not to mention slightly paranoid), but I guess I was ready for anything. I felt like that scene from Dead Man Walking, and with each step I prayed. Amazingly, by the time I reached the office, I felt a strange sense of peace. Like, okay God, You just go ahead and do whatever You like. I can handle it now.

"Here I am," I called into Mrs. King's office.

She was on the phone, but waved me in and motioned for me to sit.

She hung up the phone and turned around and smiled. "Good news, Chloe."

"Really?" I sat up straight. "What?"

"Do you know Marty Ruez?"

"I don't exactly know her, but I know who she is."

She nodded. "Well, she came forward yesterday."

"Came forward?"

"As a witness."

"A witness to what?"

"The altercation between you and Tiffany and Kerry."

"But she wasn't even—"

"She said she was hiding around the corner. She said she does that a lot. She ducks into the alcove behind Mr. Thompson's office and hides until Tiffany and her friends leave the choir room and head to lunch. It's her way to avoid the teasing that often takes place if she's walking in front of them."

I nodded. "Yeah, I've seen them do that."

"Anyway, she heard the whole thing. And she wrote it all out as an affidavit for you."

"You're kidding? She did that for me?"

"Yes, and it matches almost word for word with what you told me. Not only that, but Laura told me about the incident in the bathroom earlier this year. It also matches what you said."

I sighed. "So what happens now?"

"Well, the school would really like to see this thing settled quietly and out of court. We don't need that kind of publicity. We'd like to get Kerry to drop her charges. If necessary we can gather all the parties together and go over these new findings and put some pressure on her."

"Did you give her my letter?"

"I gave it to her yesterday."

"Good. I really am sorry I hit her and about her nose and everything. And I'm trying really hard not to be mad at her and Tiffany. I don't want to hate them."

"You don't?"

"No, I know that God wants me to love every-one—even my enemies." I made a face. "But it's sure not easy."

"You're an amazing girl, Chloe. I would think that you'd really have it out for those two by now."

"If it wasn't for God, I would. Honestly, when they attacked me last fall I actually considered doing something drastic to get back at them. But that was before I invited Jesus into my heart."

"So, you're a Christian then?"

I smiled. "Yeah. It's made a huge difference."

"I can see that."

So I walked back to composition class feeling like a load of rocks had been lifted from my back. And with each step, I thanked God. I took a few

minutes to call my parents about this new devel-
opment, and afterward, I told Allie and Laura.
Then right before choir, I walked up to Marty
Ruez and thanked her. I could tell she was
uncomfortable with this attention, and it
occurred to me that she might not want Kerry and
Tiffany to know that she was the one who had
told, since they could make her life miserable.

Toward the end of fifth period I was summoned
to Mrs. King's office again. This time, Kerry was
there too. It was the first time I'd seen her up
close with her bandaged nose, and I could see now
that her eyes were also blackened. Man, I must've
really walloped her good.

"I'm sorry, Kerry," I said as soon as I saw her.

She nodded. "It's okay. I guess I was asking for
it."

"Why don't you both sit down," said Mrs. King.
Then she turned toward me. "Kerry and I have
been talking this whole thing through, and she's
willing to drop all charges."

Kerry looked down at the floor. "I didn't really
want to press charges in the first place. It was
Tiffany's idea, and then she got my parents all
worked up and, well, it just sort of mushroomed."

Mrs. King nodded. "I told Kerry about the witnesses who had already prepared affidavits and
were willing to testify against her."

I looked at Kerry. "Did you read my letter?"

"Yeah," she said without looking up. "Thanks."

The office was silent for a moment then Mrs. King cleared her throat. "Uh, Kerry, was there something you wanted to say to Chloe?"

Kerry looked up. "Yeah."

I waited.

"Well, it was wrong for me and Tiffany to pick on you." She slowly shook her head. "I don't even know how that whole thing got started in the first place. I guess I was afraid Tiffany would quit being my friend if I didn't go along with her. She can turn on people really quickly, you know. And, well, it doesn't matter now anyway since she's not going to be my friend anymore."

"I know it's probably wrong to say this, Kerry," I said, "but I think you'd be a whole lot better off without her."

She looked down again. "Yeah, maybe."

"I plan to speak to Tiffany this afternoon," said Mrs. King. "This incident will also go on her record."

"So what happens now?" I asked. "I mean, with the police and everything?"

"Kerry and her family will have to straighten that up. And you'll want them to talk to your attorney, Chloe."

"And what about here at school?" I asked. "Mr. Thompson probably still thinks I instigated the whole thing."

"I'm going to insist that Tiffany and Kerry tell him the truth," said Mrs. King. "That you were defending yourself. And, don't worry; I'll follow it up too."

"So, is this it then?"

She smiled. "Pretty much. I just hope you girls learned something through all this."

Kerry nodded sadly. And I said, "I think so, but I'm still processing everything."

And even tonight I feel as though I'm still trying to wrap my mind around what happened during the past three days. I mean, it's like one moment everything is going just fine—couldn't be better—then the next moment your whole world is caving in on top of you. But I guess life is just like that. Whether you have God in your life or not, stuff is going to happen. The difference is in how you handle it when it does. If you're trusting in God and asking Him for help, things turn out better. At least that's how it seems to me. Because I'm thinking if this whole thing had happened before I asked God into my life, well, I'm sure I could've been in all kinds of trouble. Maybe I would be in jail right now; I don't know.

My dad is still pretty mad about the whole thing and keeps saying he wants Mr. Collier to sue both those girls for slander and assault and who knows what else. But I keep telling him to just chill. Still, he says he's going to make them pay for our legal costs (which can't be much since Mr. Collier only spent an hour or so with us). I told my dad he should just forgive and forget, and he laughed and said, "Now, don't go taking this religion thing too far, Chloe." So I thought I'd better leave it at that for now. No sense beating him over the head with it.

FORGIVING
to forgive isn't cheap
it doesn't come free
it costs pride and face
and memory
it's biding your time
and biting your tongue
and forgetting words
carelessly slung
Jesus forgave
He paid in full
He'll show us how
and make us whole
if we just trust
and learn to live
as we're forgiven
is how to forgive
cm

Thursday, December 12

I played at the Paradiso again tonight—to a full house. A lot of kids from school were there including Torrey and Cortney, and to my surprise even Kerry showed up. Not with Tiffany, of course, since those two are sworn enemies these days (or so I've heard). But Kerry was with her new boyfriend and seemed happy. She and I actually have a casual talking relationship now. It's weird how things can change so quickly. And, of course, my friends were there sitting at one of the front tables and cheering and jeering me on. Also, Mr. Thompson was there with his wife. That was kinda cool. He came up afterward and shook my hand and told me that it was a great performance.

So it sort of feels as if life is returning to normal—if there is such a thing, and I like to think there isn't. Because what is normal anyway? To me the word is the same as boring. And who wants that? Still, I don't mind having a little less chaos these days. Life with God can be exciting enough without the threat of lawsuits and jail hanging over your head.

Speaking of exciting I'm involved in five different musical performances this month. Two are related to choir, two with the coffeehouse, and one with church. Pretty cool! And I'm saving up

my money toward the possibility of cutting a CD.
But I'm still not sure if I should go solo on it or
do it with our "band." Although we're not calling
ourselves an official band yet. And we still don't
have a name. I'm praying that God will make it
clear—and that He'll open the doors as needed.

Pastor Tony was talking about how God can
either open or close doors for us. And we need to
remember that just because a door gets closed, we
shouldn't get discouraged because it might be
saving us from something that wouldn't be good
for us. But he also said that just because a door
is wide open doesn't mean we should walk right
through it.

I kind of struggle with that because when I
see an open door (especially one that looks inviting) I want to just walk right in and make myself
at home. But Tony said that we need a whole set of
checks and balances like reading God's Word and
listening to good advice, and we need to make
sure all these things line up and point in the
same direction. And I suppose that makes sense,
although I do like the idea of just walking right
through an open door. Still, who knows what
might lurk ahead even when something looks
good? So I'm praying that God will help me to be
wise.

                    BEHIND THE DOOR
                      an open door
                      an invitation
                       to come in
                      no explanation
                       is it right
                      or is it wrong?
                        set apart
                       or belong
                      unseeing eyes
                      deafened ears
                       yield to pain
                       end in tears
                       make me wise
                      make me strong
                       to follow You
                     my whole life long
                         amen
                          cm

Monday, December 16

Totally cool night. Unforgettable even. We had a candlelit Christmas concert at the church. And it was beautiful.

But first let me share the big news. We are officially a band now. I know this is going to sound weird, but I had a dream last week—a really vivid dream—and we three girls were playing on a big stage with lights and a huge sound system and what seemed like thousands of people in the audience. It was so awesome. And our band had a name: Redemption.

Well, when I woke up it seemed so real—it felt as though God had given me the dream, and I was so excited I couldn't even go back to sleep. So the next day I told Laura and Allie about it. I was all prepared for them to roll their eyes and call me a nutcase and basically just hate the idea altogether. But they both got real quiet then almost simultaneously shouted, "That's it!" So anyway, we knew we had this church gig coming up in just a few days, and we decided to make the big announcement then.

So tonight I introduced us by saying, "My name is Chloe and these are my friends Laura and Allie, and we have just officially become a band." The audience clapped politely. "And for the first time anywhere we are announcing our official band name. It's Redemption." And then the audience clapped even louder. We played our first song and the audience clapped with real enthusiasm, and they seemed to like our other songs too.

And so Redemption is officially launched today. We're even going to check into registering our name with a trademark or something, if it's not too expensive. I'll talk to Mr. Collier about this. Also, I've decided that if I save up enough money to cut a CD, I'll do it with the band, not solo. It just seems right.

OUR BIRTH ANNOUNCEMENT
a band was born tonight
on december 16th
making its appearance at 7:42 p.m.
weighing in at several hundred pounds
its Father is God
and its name is Redemption
keep it in your prayers
cm

Monday, December 23

An amazing thing has happened in our family. My brother Josh has (sort of...) become engaged. To Caitlin, of course! Well, they don't exactly call it an engagement. I think Josh said it's a covenant, but it sounds like an engagement to me. He even gave her a ring. Now my parents like Caitlin a lot, but I don't think they were overly thrilled with the whole thing. In fact, I think my dad's just trying to blow the whole thing off, as if it's nothing more serious than going steady. But, knowing Josh and Caitlin, I think it's more serious than that.

And like I've said before, it's plain to see those two are in love. At least it's plain to me. Although I think they're a little young (I personally wouldn't want to get married until I was at least twenty-five!), I do think it's pretty cool. I would love to have Caitlin as my sister-in-law. She already seems like a sister to me. So, I told them I thought it was great.

I really admire them too. They've both made this commitment to God to keep their relationship "pure." That's what Josh calls it. They've both promised to abstain from sex until they're actually married. I think that's a bit unusual these days. But maybe it makes sense when you think of how people get hurt in relationships all the time, and I'm guessing sex usually has a lot to do with it.

I know how it was with me just about a year ago when a certain boyfriend was pressuring me. And that whole thing ended up in such a mess—and I got deeply hurt. All because I wouldn't go along with him. And I suppose, in some ways, that was when things started changing for me. I pulled away from my friends (since they were all gossiping about me) and more into myself. I started dressing and acting differently—maybe just to rebel against the norm. I'm still not totally sure. And it's not as if I'm saying that everything that came out of that era was completely bad or good; it was just different, change, transition. In fact, looking back now, I think God actually used that whole sequence of events to start bringing me to Him.

Still, I'm not sure that I'm ready to make any

big commitments about sex at the moment—one
way or another. To be honest, it's not something
that even interests me much right now—there's
too much else going on in my life. I suppose if I
had a real serious boyfriend, I might have to
think harder about this whole thing. But, hey, I'm
in no big hurry to have sex—as if anyone's even
asking! I guess it's something I'll have to work
out between God and me. In due time that is. And I
mean His time, not mine.

YOUR TIME
when it's time
You will show
i will be
the first to know
until then
i will wait
on You Lord
and contemplate
just how much
i love You
and to Your heart
i'll be true
all i want
is Your best
i can wait
for the rest
cm

Christmas Day, December 25

I took some time by myself this afternoon, to take a walk and just talk to God—alone and undisturbed by tinsel and trees and jingle bells (not that I don't like those things because I really do!). As odd as it probably seemed to any casual observers, especially on Christmas, I went up to the cemetery—to my rebirth place. I just wanted some quiet time to think about what He has done for me—for us. How He came to earth in the form of a vulnerable little baby—His Son—to show us how much He loved us.

As I walked around the familiar gravestones, I wondered if I would be willing to do something so huge, like leave the comfort of a wonderful place like heaven to go someplace cold and dark and foreboding. I considered Katherine Lucinda dancing with the angels in the warm golden light up above (or whatever it is they do up there), and I'm sure it must be fantastic. Anyway, I thanked Jesus for doing this thing—for coming to earth—for loving me, and for changing my life.

Just a year ago I was totally miserable. I didn't even know what the point of Christmas was. And I remember getting into a huge fight with my parents, and I actually considered running away on Christmas Eve. I wanted to hurt them because they seemed so stupid and shallow and hypocritical to me at the time.

And now, well, I suppose they haven't really changed, but even so it's easier to accept them for who they are. And I know that's God at work in me. I mean, we're all different—that's how God made us—and it's okay. So, I guess I'm the one who's changed the most. And just taking some time to consider these things makes me so thankful. I wonder what I'll be feeling by next Christmas.

WONDER OF WONDERS
oh, God, what You have done
leaving the comfort and beauty
the perfection of heaven
to come down here
to our darkness, our filth, our hopelessness
oh, what You gave up
for us
pouring Your Godself into the tiny vessel
of a fragile child
oh, wonder of wonders
i stand here amazed
at Your awesome love
and i thank You again
and again
amen
cm

Sixteen

Saturday, January 4

We had an extra long practice today since we're going to play at the Paradiso Café next Friday night—our first paying gig as a band. Which also managed to launch us into our first major disagreement since Allie has become a Christian. It's like the honeymoon was over. Or maybe just the roller coaster taking a sharp plunge. Anyway, I had just suggested that we should put our earnings (which won't be much) toward making a CD. "We could even open a savings account in our band's name."

"Yeah," agreed Laura. "That's cool."

"Hey, wait a minute," said Allie. "Do I get a vote here?"

"Of course." I turned to see what she had to say.

"It's all good and well for you two to decide to put our earnings into a savings account," she began, juggling her drumsticks as she talked. "But Laura, you have a job, and Chloe, you have rich parents. So it's no big deal to you. But for me to earn a few bucks and actually get to keep it, well, that's something I was kinda looking forward to."

So we kicked it around for a while, and I hate to admit it, but it got a little hot in there (and I don't mean the temperature). I just didn't see why Allie wasn't willing to reinvest this money back into the band.

"Look, Allie," I reminded her, "You're not doing so badly. You've got a roof over your head and food to eat and clothes to wear. What more do you need?"

"That's easy for you to say!" She hit her cymbal hard. "You've got it made here on Snob Hill."

"Hey, that's not fair—"

"And I don't have it as good as Chloe," injected Laura. "But you don't see me holding back."

"You've got a job—"

"I work hard at my job. It's not like they're handing me the money on a silver platter!"

And so it went. Finally, after Allie had burst into tears and both Laura and I had to apologize, we decided it was time to pray. That's when we made a really good discovery. See, good things do come out of bad (when you allow God to lead, that is). We discovered that as a band we needed to put God first.

"I think we should always start practice by praying together," said Laura as we were packing up.

"Yeah, that'd be good," agreed Allie.

"And maybe we should write something down," I suggested.

"Huh?" Allie looked at me. "You mean like a contract?"

"Not exactly. Well, maybe. Kind of like a contract between God and us. Something that clearly says what we are about—what our purpose as a band is."

Laura nodded. "I like that."

"Me too," said Allie. "But let's not make it too complicated. Stuff never works when it's too complicated. Like when I was twelve, some friends and I tried to start a club, but the rules were so hard to remember that we finally just gave it all up."

"Yeah," I agreed, "let's keep it simple."

So we sat down and put our heads together and finally came up with our list. (My dad says it's called a mission statement.) Anyway, it's not terribly original. Mostly, it's just what Jesus said. But as simple as it sounds, it took us about an hour to agree on it. This is what it is:

1) Put God first in our lives
2) Love each other
3) Glorify God in our music

Sunday, January 12

Our gig at the Paradiso was a real hit on Friday night. The place was packed full with SRO (standing room only). And Laura and Allie played better than ever. I actually found myself wondering what I could've been thinking when I'd seriously considered the whole "going solo" biz. I mean, I might be pretty good on my own, but I think we're totally awesome as a group. Of course, that's only my humble opinion.

My parents were there too, along with their friends the Stephensens. Afterward Mr. Stephensen came up and talked to us.

"You girls have really got something here."

"Thanks, Mr. Stephensen," I said. "This is Laura and Allie."

He smiled and shook their hands. "Just call me Ron."

"Ron teaches music at the college," I explained.

"Yeah, and this isn't the first time I've told Chloe that she's onto something with her music here. You girls could have a future."

"Really?" Allie's eyes grew big. "You mean professionally?"

"I'm not a real expert, but I know when someone has potential. Are you girls really serious about your music?"

"We practice a lot," said Laura.

"It shows." He handed me a business card. "If you're still interested in cutting a CD, give me a call. You'll never get anywhere without a CD."

"Yeah, that's what Willy says too," said Allie.

"Willy?"

"He gives me drumming lessons. He used to tour with a rock band."

He nodded. "Well, he's right. It takes a lot to make it in the music business, but cutting a CD is the first step." He started to leave then stopped. "Hey, have you entered the Battle of the Bands?"

"Battle of the Bands?" I asked. "What's that?"

"I hope it's not too late." He scratched his head. "It's up at the college. There's a twenty-five-dollar entry fee, but it's great exposure for picking up local gigs. They even give out some prizes."

"How do we sign up?" I asked.

"Why don't you let me look into it for you," he suggested. "I could even sign you up."

I looked at Laura and Allie. "You want to?" I could tell by Allie's face that she was calculating her third of the entry fee. "I'll cover the twenty-five bucks," I said quietly.

"I'm in," Allie said with a bright smile.

"Me too," added Laura.

"Okay, then." I shook Ron's hand. "See if you can get us in."

He called the next day while we were practicing and said he pulled a couple strings and we're
in! The whole thing happens next Saturday. So we
decided to practice both Saturday and Sunday as
well as three nights next week.

"You know what the grand prize is?" I said,
directing my question to Allie.

Her eyes lit up. "A million bucks?"

"No, silly. It's a brand-new, really good PEARL
drum set!"

"You're kidding?" She clutched her drumsticks. "Do you think we really have a chance?"

"Ron does."

Laura cleared her throat. "Yeah, but if we win,
I suppose we'd have to sell the drum set and split
the money three ways."

"Yeah, or put it all toward cutting our CD," I
added, turning to wink at Laura.

Allie slumped down and groaned. "You mean
you guys would sell a perfectly good drum set?"

"You're always complaining about wanting
money," Laura reminded her. "That would put some
cash in your pocket."

"But..." Allie just shook her head.

"Oh, I don't know. What do you think, Laura,
could we let her keep the drums?"

"I suppose it wouldn't hurt. And the whole
band would benefit from it. No offense, Chloe, but
your brother's drums are a little cheesy."

"Hey, watch what you're calling cheesy," warned Allie, pretending to hug the bass drum. "I like these guys."

"Oh, well, then, maybe we'll just sell the new set after all."

"Not so fast." Allie stood up. "I think Redemption could use a better sounding set of drums."

"I'll say!"

"You mean if we win," Laura reminded us.

"And that's a big if," I added.

"Let's get to work!" Allie sat back down and started hitting the beat for the next song on our list.

And so now we're all praying that somehow, someway, we'll get that first prize and take home that drum set for Allie—well, for all of us, really.

> is it wrong to want success
> to ask God if He will bless?
> is it selfishness or greed
> to have a goal, to succeed?
> is it wrong when we expect
> fame or fortune, benefit?
> just because God's our Dad
> shouldn't mean we have it bad
> can't we ask for something more
> that He'll open up a door?

> after all, He is King
> He can do anything!
> cm

Thursday, January 16

Bad news. We just found out that Screaming Tangerine is going to be at the Battle of the Bands. All the kids at school are talking about it. Screaming Tangerine is a local band that everyone predicts is about to make it big time. It almost seems unfair that they get to compete. But then I suppose they'll bring in a lot of ticket sales, and the whole purpose of the concert is to raise money for the college music program. Oh, well. At least we get to compete. That'll be fun.

Allie was pretty down about the whole thing at lunch today. But Laura kept assuring her that we still have a chance. I'm not so sure, but for Allie's sake I'm acting as if we could still win.

But here's what is fun. Word's gotten around school that we're going to be in the Battle of the Bands, and some people are actually treating us like celebrities. Allie really eats this kind of attention up. And even though Laura acts as though it's no big deal, I can tell she loves it too. I'm not quite sure how to act exactly, but I try not to gloat when I see someone like Tiffany Knight scowling at me in choir. She doesn't put me down anymore, but she's not what you'd call civil either. In fact, I'm sure this whole thing totally irks her. And I try not to take too much satisfaction in that, but, hey, I _am_ human. Sorry, God. Help me to be kinder.

I TOOK A RIDE
upon my pride
it started out real fun
i went fast
and had a blast
and waved at everyone
but down the hill
i took a spill
went spinning into space
i hit a bump
and took a lump
got mud upon my face
whoooops!
cm

Saturday, January 18

What a night! My head is still spinning. Okay, this is what happened. They let the bands draw numbers for when they played, and we got number sixteen (and that was out of eighteen bands). So we had to sit there and sweat and freak and chew our nails down to the nubbins while _fifteen_ other great bands performed before us.

Okay, I'll admit that some of the bands weren't all that great, and I felt pretty sure that we could easily beat some of them. But some of them were really good too. Like Fat Tango—another girls' band that was really hot and got huge applause. And most of the bands have been playing together for years (not just a few months!). And, of course, Screaming Tangerine performed about midway through the concert, and the crowd absolutely went wild for them, stomping and clapping for an encore, which the emcee practically guaranteed when he said, "Hey, don't worry; the winning band will play again at the end of the show."

"Screaming Tangerine is obviously in first now," Allie told us with a glum face. "And Blue Night is probably tied with Fat Tango, with Chop-Shop not too far behind."

We both nodded. That sounded about right. We sat there and pretended to enjoy the music when I know that all we could think about was getting this thing over with and getting out of there. Then just as the band before us was playing and we were waiting backstage, Allie started to freeze up.

"I can't do this," she said. "I'm gonna be sick."

"Come on, Al," I urged her. "Just take a deep breath and relax. It's no different than playing the Paradiso."

And then she threw up—all over my guitar. Okay, I'll admit that for a split second I wanted to kill her. Maybe for a few seconds. Then I grabbed my denim jacket and tried to wipe the gluck off and dry my guitar. I heard a guy behind us totally losing it as if we were the funniest thing on the planet. Laura made Allie take some drinks from her water bottle and gently wiped down her face then said, "You better just shape up, girl-friend!" She glared at her. "Cuz we're going out there, and we're not taking any excuses from anyone! Understand?"

Allie just nodded, and when it was our turn, we both grabbed a hand and literally dragged her out. We tried to smile and laugh, as if it were all just a big act. But then I looked Allie in the eye and actually said a quick prayer. "God be with us!" I let go of her hand and walked over to the mike and started to speak.

"My name is Chloe, and my friend on bass over there is Laura. And the drummer who just barfed all over my guitar is Allie." Well, this really cracked them up, and I think it gave Allie a moment to gather her wits.

"And we are Redemption!" I shouted, then turned and looked at Allie. I swear her face was white as chalk, but she started counting out the beat and then we played. Okay, we didn't play our best—thanks to Allie's stage fright—but at least we tried. And we didn't make complete fools of ourselves. The crowd actually seemed to like us— a lot. Or else they just felt sorry for us. I'm sure we were the youngest ones there, and the whole barfing thing must've sounded pretty pitiful.

I was just glad to be done with it. And as soon as we finished, I marched off to the bathroom to clean up my guitar. What a stench! To be honest, I was glad to have an excuse to get away. I was still pretty ticked at Allie, and I didn't want to say something I'd regret. Like, "Thanks for helping me throw away twenty-five bucks!"

By the time I got back out there, the last band was performing. They were really pretty lame, but the crowd was generous and clapped anyway. But you could tell it was only polite clapping. Then the emcee came out again and started chattering away about everything from the weather to politics, trying to be funny. But by then nothing seemed funny to me; I just wanted to go home and forget about tonight.

So finally he's announcing who the winners are, starting with third place, which turned out to be Fat Tango. I actually clapped and cheered now because I really thought they were good. They went up and received their award, a check for two hundred and fifty dollars. Not bad considering it was only third. Then the emcee said, "Now for second place. Hey, it looks like it's ladies night tonight. Will the band with the barfing drummer—<u>Redemption</u>—come on up here?"

Well, I thought I was going to faint. I grabbed Laura's arm. "Did he say—?"

"It's us!" she screamed. "Come on, Allie!" Laura gave her a shove toward the stairs then tugged on me. "Come on, you guys! Let's move it!"

And the next thing I knew, I was up there saying thanks and receiving a check for five hundred dollars!!! Laura was hysterical and Allie was in tears.

"Did the drummer really barf on your guitar?" the emcee asked.

I nodded soberly. "Yeah, I was just in the bathroom cleaning it all off. Man, you shoulda smelled it!" Well, the audience went into hysterics over that.

Then, of course, Screaming Tangerine was presented with first place and got back on stage for an encore, which we enjoyed immensely. Afterward, we were getting our pictures taken and the drummer from Tangerine told me they would've rather had the check since his drum set was even better than the prize. Then I told him that our barfing drummer had been really hoping for a new drum set. "You should see the one she has to play on at home."

"You wanna trade?" he said, but I thought he was joking.

"Oh, yeah, sure." I turned and smiled for another photo.

Then just as we were getting ready to go, the leader of their band, Scott Cinder, walked up to me. "You guys serious about wanting to trade prizes?"

"Are you kidding?" I stared at him.

"What's up?" asked Laura. I quickly told her what they were saying, and she said, "Why not? If they're serious."

So before Allie even realized what had happened we switched prizes.

"We're just hitting the road now," said Scott. "We don't have time to deal with trying to sell those drums, and we could really use some extra cash. Besides, we thought it would be kinda cool to be known as the guys who helped out the barfing drummer on an up-and-coming band." He smiled. "You guys are really good."

And so there you have it! What an unbelievable night. Allie just about passed out when we told her what we'd done. Well, at first she didn't even believe us.

"You guys are just trying to get even with me for messing up tonight," she said. "And I don't even blame you. I'm so embarrassed. I'm sorry."

But when we showed her the certificate for the Right Chord music store and convinced her it was for real, she just started shaking.

"I can't believe it," she said. "I cannot believe it! Scott Cinder really said that?"

So go figure. Allie lost it and barfed on my guitar, but we still came in second. And even though we came in second, we still walked home with the prize for first. Now, I am thinking that only God could do something that impossible.

DESPITE US
despite who we are
all our fragilities, inabilities
You showed up
despite our ineptness
our comedy of errors
You came through
despite us
our doubts and our fears
You carried us along
thank You
amen
cm

Seventeen

Wednesday, February 5

Life seems to have slowed down during the last couple weeks. I suppose that's good. I'm sure my parents were getting worried that all this success was going to go straight to our heads, like maybe we'd hit the road with our show. Ha! I could just see us piling into Laura's little Neon (which isn't even paid for yet) with all our equipment and stuff and trying to make it to Nashville or New York or wherever it is that bands go to hit it big these days.

But we do have a date to cut a CD now. Hopefully with our next two coffeehouse gigs, plus playing for a birthday party that Laura booked for us, we'll have enough to cover the cost. If not, my dad promised to help us out. And Ron Stephensen said that he'd give us the best deal he could in the studio. Willy's been working with us lately too. Kind of mentoring, I guess you'd say.

We don't agree with everything he suggests, but he's got some good advice and seems to know a lot about the music business. Although sometimes it seems as though he's trying to scare us out of trying to do too much. "They'll chew you up alive," he likes to say. "And then spit you out again." But I'm thinking if God wants us to do something big, well, then He can make it happen, and He can protect us from the ones who would try to hurt us. In the meantime, I think we need to just focus on doing our best right here and now. Who knows what lies ahead? Besides God, that is.

                    WHAT'S NEXT?
                    i close my eyes
                  and dream a dream
                about what lies ahead
                   amazing things
                  songs and lights
               all play across my bed
                  but what is real
                  and what is not
              and what will be will be
                   i cannot tell
                  i cannot guess
             what lies in store for me
               (but i trust You, God)
                      amen

Sunday, February 16

Well, I guess I've been a little self-absorbed lately, what with music and friends and church and all. But I just got the strangest e-mail from

Caitlin today. I didn't even know what to think of it. She and Josh were pretty much engaged at Christmastime, and as far as I knew everything was just fine. But now she has called it all off. I was stunned. And sad. She didn't give me any details, so I called her up and asked what was going on.

"It's a long story, Chloe." Her voice sounded so far away and tired.

"That's okay. I have time. If you want to tell me, that is."

She sighed. "Well, I know you'll understand if I tell you it's a God-thing. And more than anything else, I want to obey God. Does that make sense?"

"Sure, that's what I want too. But are you saying God doesn't want you to marry Josh?"

"All I know for right now is that I'm not supposed to be committed to Josh like that. For right now, I need to just wait on God and obey Him."

"Then maybe later—"

"I don't know about later, Chloe. I can't see into the future."

"Is there another guy?"

Then she laughed and I felt relieved. "No, of course not."

"Do you still love Josh?"

"Yes, of course. I never quit loving him. I just can't promise to marry him. It was really messing me up. It's like I was all depressed and confused, and finally God showed me that we jumped the gun. I never should've agreed to that whole thing."

"Does Josh understand all this?"

"I'm not sure."

"Well, he knows, doesn't he?"

"Yeah. He knows." Her voice sounded flat, or maybe it was just sad.

"Is he okay?"

"I don't know."

"Are you okay?"

"I think I will be. It's just so soon. Like I'm still sort of in shock. But actually, once it was done I did start to feel better—as if I could sense God's presence in my life again."

"Really? You mean being engaged to Josh took God out of your life? But Josh is a Christian and a—"

"It doesn't have to do with Josh. You're right; he's the best. The very best." She paused now. "It had to do with me trusting God completely and being willing to be 100 percent obedient to Him—even if it was the hardest thing I've ever had to do."

"Was it really the hardest?"

"I think so."

"So, you really still love Josh then?"

"Yes. But, Chloe, please keep this between you and me."

"You know you can trust me," I assured her.
And then I told her I'd be praying for her and
Josh too and that I thought God would work it all
out for both of them. Of course, I'm thinking that
means God will work it out for them to eventually
get married—because that's what I think is going
to happen. But I didn't tell Caitlin that. I could
tell it wasn't what she needed to hear right now. I
just hope Josh doesn't get too depressed with this
news. I'll be praying especially hard for him.
Poor guy.

This reminds of what Caitlin has said all
along about dating. She said that no matter how
you do it, someone always gets hurt. I'm starting
to wonder if maybe she's right. Still, I haven't
even had much opportunity to go there myself,
and I'm not eager to go closing doors—unless God
wants me to, that is.

HOLD THEM BOTH
o, Lord, keep them in Your hand
give them peace and help them stand
cover them with lots of grace
let them see Your tender face
wrap Your arms of love around
keep them safe and keep them sound
amen
cm

Saturday, February 22

We cut our first CD today. Notice I say "first" as if I think we may someday cut another. Well, who knows? It could happen. Ron Stephensen thinks it could. And so does Willy. Despite Willy's occasional gloom-and-doom forecasts about the music industry in general, he's usually quite optimistic when it comes to our talent and potential.

"You just need the right connections," he said today as we were loading our stuff into his van. "I keep praying that God will send the right people along for you—when the time is right."

I laughed. "You mean, like someone to discover us?"

"Yeah, that's pretty much what it takes."

I guess the truly amazing thing is that we managed to do it all in one day—one very long day. Okay, it's not a perfect CD. And if we'd had a couple weeks (and a couple hundred thousand bucks), I think it would've been much better. At least that's what Willy said. But then it's just a demo. Hopefully anyone who hears it will understand that.

Just as we were leaving the recording studio I remembered something. "Hey, I forgot to tell you guys that this coffeehouse over in Lake View wants us to play during spring break. It's a

Christian place called the Samaritan. I went there last year with a friend. It's funny because I wasn't even a Christian then, and now they want us to come play."

"Sounds good to me," said Laura. "I'm not going anywhere for spring break. In fact, I promised to work for my aunt all week. What day is it?"

"It's a Saturday. As I recall, the place is about three times as big as Paradiso so there could be a fairly good-sized crowd."

"Is this a paying gig?" asked Allie.

"Yeah, but only a hundred bucks. Still, the guy said we could sell our CDs and make some extra money that way. Ron said we should have them by then."

So we started talking about designing some kind of cover for our CD. And before long we were arguing about whether to use a graphic design or a photograph.

"Look, I think you guys should let me do it," said Allie.

"Well, you are the most artistic one," said Laura.

"Yeah, but we all have to agree on it," I added. "Don't go printing off a bunch of covers without showing it to us first."

"Like I would do that."

>
                    YOUR WAY
                show us Your way
              set the path before us
              and teach us to walk
               help us to trust You
              and hold to Your hand
                 we don't know
                 which way to go
                  without You
                show us Your way
                    amen
                     cm

Saturday, March 1

This morning my dad was walking around the
house whistling and all happy, and I asked what
was up.

"I'm thinking about booking a family trip for
us during spring break."

I frowned. "Really?"

"What's wrong with that? I thought we could
get one of those good deals on a Caribbean cruise.
And Josh could come too. It would be fun. You
know there's probably not going to be many more
family vacations with you kids growing up."

I controlled myself from saying that it might
be a good thing since our family vacations most
often ended up in big family fights. "Do you think

we could be back by the twenty-eighth?"

"What's going on then?"

"Well, we kinda had a gig set up."

My dad rolled his eyes. "Chloe, you'll have your whole life to do music gigs if you want to, but this might be our last chance to do something like this all together."

"All together?" I raised my brows. "You mean the whole family is going?"

Okay, I know that was a low blow and probably undeserved. But sometimes I just want to jerk my parents' chain a little when it comes to my oldest brother, Caleb. I mean, I get tired of them pretending he's dead or something. It's as if they won't even talk about it. The only one I can talk about it with is Josh, and he's hardly ever around. But at least Josh and I are praying for Caleb. And I really believe that someday Caleb is going to figure things out and that he'll let God into his life and come back to his family. In the meantime, I just pray that he's safe. It scares me to think about it too much. I realize that he's probably living a dangerous life. And sometimes I think he could be in real trouble—or even dead—and we wouldn't even know about it. Then I have to pray really hard!

Well, anyway, my comment about Caleb pretty much put a damper on my dad this morning. And for that I felt bad. I hadn't meant to rain on his parade. Not really. And who knows, maybe a cruise would be a good thing for Josh. Even though he acts like it's all just fine and dandy, I know he's still hurting from Caitlin's breakup.

So later this evening when I saw my dad intently searching the Net, perusing the travel networks for good cruise deals, I didn't say anything negative. In fact, I just pretended not to notice.

But now I'm thinking, am I crazy? Why am I willing to pass up a perfectly good Caribbean cruise just to stay home and play at a coffeehouse? But I am. I realized right away that I shouldn't mention the possibility of any of this to Laura and Allie. For one thing, I'm the one who set up the coffeehouse gig in the first place. But besides that, I can just hear Allie digging into me for giving up an opportunity like that. She'd kill to go on a cruise. Okay, not kill, since that would be wrong. Anyway, I kept my mouth closed about this during practice today.

Just as we were quitting, Allie did a little drumroll (on her new and very cool drum set). "I have an announcement to make." She pulled out a folder. "The artwork for our new CD cover is ready for your approval."

Laura and I went over to get a closer look, waiting for her to unveil her creation.

"Here it is!" She held up what looked to be a

collage and upon closer inspection was really quite good. She'd taken a photo of us (from the night she'd barfed on my guitar), pasted it along with some other things, and then done some drawing with ink on top and written the word Redemption in scraggly red letters.

"This is really cool, Allie," I said. "I can see this as a CD cover."

"I don't know..." Laura frowned. "It's so edgy looking. Is that really the image we want?"

We both turned and looked at Laura. I think it was one of the few times when I really saw Laura the way most people probably see her. I guess I sort of think of myself as not really looking on the exterior of people so much. Oh, I know I have my hang-ups—particularly with people who look too perfect—but for the most part, I try not to put too much stock into appearances. But just then, as Laura was making this statement about image, it hit me: She looks pretty much like a preppy. An African-American preppy chick. Then I turned and looked at Allie. I have to admit I think I've had an influence on her looks, because she dresses kind of like me now. Kind of grunge or urban or I-couldn't-care-less-what-you-think kind of look. And I think she looks pretty cool.

Then we were both looking at Laura, and I think we both had the same expression on our faces.

"What?" demanded Laura defensively.

"I don't know..." I shrugged. "I guess I never really thought we had to have an image."

Laura firmly shook her head. "No way. I don't buy that. You get up every day and you look in the mirror and then dress like a bum, and now you're saying you don't think we need to have an image?"

I laughed. "You think I dress like a bum?"

She nodded. "Well, what do you expect me or anyone else to think, for that matter? You both are into this look. But I'm sorry; it's not for everyone. And it's definitely not for me."

"Sheesh, Laura." I scratched my head. "It's like you've really given this some thought."

She walked over to the other side of the room and sank down onto the old couch against the wall and just sighed.

We followed her over there. Allie perched on a couch arm, I flopped onto the floor, and we both just looked at her. "Does the way we look really bother you?" I asked.

She shrugged.

"Come on, tell us the truth," urged Allie.

"Yeah, sure it bothers me."

"Why didn't you tell us this before?" I asked.

She pushed the sleeves of her sweater up and leaned forward. "Well, at first when we first started jamming, I told myself it didn't matter. I mean, I thought you were a really good musician,

Chloe, and I just wanted to play with you for fun, hoping that I'd get better. I didn't seriously think we'd become a real band. And besides, I knew you weren't a Christian to start out, and Allie was all into her witchcraft stuff, and I guess as time passed and things changed, I figured that eventually—" she waved her hands and rolled her eyes—"you guys would just change too."

I had to laugh. "But haven't we?"

"Of course you've changed, but you still look just as ratty as ever. In fact, Allie looks worse."

"Hey, thanks a lot." Allie frowned.

"So what are we supposed to do now?" I asked.

"I don't know." She looked at us. "I guess I'm really the odd one out here."

"Do you think Allie and I should change to look like you?"

She shook her head. "No, that's probably not fair."

"And I don't think we should force you to look like us," I said.

"Thanks."

"So maybe we should change our name to Preppy and the Rats," I suggested.

This made her laugh. "No, I like our name, and I actually think Allie's cover looks pretty cool. But I do think it's weird when we perform and look like we belong in two different groups."

"It doesn't bother me."

"Me neither," added Allie.

"Okay, then it bothers me. I guess I'm the image-conscious one of the group."

I shrugged. "I don't think it matters that much, Laura. I've seen groups where everyone looks different. It's just who they are."

"But maybe I don't want to be different!" And then for the first time ever, we saw Laura cry.

We both sat on the couch and put our arms around her. "We're all different, Laura," I said. "That's what makes us work so good together. It's how God made us."

"I know." She sniffed. "But it's not fair; I'm different already. I'm black, if you haven't noticed, and you guys are pretty white. I guess I just don't want to be totally different, you know?"

"So what are you saying?" asked Allie.

"Well, maybe I should try to look a little more like you guys—just for when we perform. I'm not going to go to school looking all, you know—"

"Ratty," I filled in for her.

"Yeah, whatever."

"So how can we help?" I asked. "You want us to loan you some ratty clothes?"

Allie giggled. "That ratty word just kills me."

"And I'm not piercing anything," Laura warned us.

"No one wants you to." Allie put her hand on

Laura's straightened hair. "But can we mess up your hair a little?"

Laura smiled. "Just as long as you don't use scissors."

"All right then," said Allie. "I think we can make you look almost as ratty as us."

So we went up to my closet and found some clothes that Laura was willing to wear for our next gig. "Can I be in charge of Laura's new look?" asked Allie, her eyes bright with excitement.

"Sure, I don't care. Just don't pressure her into something she doesn't like." I patted Laura on the back. "I really want to respect your individuality here. I guess it kind of bugs me that you feel the need to change your image. You sure about this?"

She nodded. "It's been bugging me for a long time. But I kept thinking you guys would change." Then she grinned. "To tell you the truth, it seems as if you're the ones who look the most like musicians anyway. And I suppose underneath my little preppy exterior I was plain jealous."

"Hey, as long as you're happy," I said. "I'm cool."

So, I guess it's settled. Although I still feel a little uneasy. And if Laura changes her mind and wants to stick with her preppy look, I'll be happy. I don't like the idea of someone changing her look just to fit in with someone else.

WHAT DO YOU SEE?
be yourself
not someone else
cuz what you see
is what you get
and what you see
is what God made
so love yourself
cuz God loves you
then you'll love others
cuz you love yourself
and you'll love God
cuz you're like Him
so be yourself
and be like God
cuz what you see
is what you get
cm

Eighteen

Monday, March 3

Today is my birthday, but I really didn't have any big expectations. I never even told anyone that it was my birthday—not that I can remember anyway. But just as I was coming out of choir, I felt someone grab me from behind. I'm sure my heart stopped for a moment because I felt certain it was Tiffany and her thugs getting ready to beat me up again. I actually wondered if I'd be able to turn the other cheek this time, but I honestly felt fairly certain I would not (and this still troubles me some...).

Fortunately it was Laura, and I began to breathe again. "Now, don't be afraid, Miss Miller," she said in a voice that I'm sure she thought I wouldn't recognize. "Just cooperate with us and no one will get hurt." Then I heard giggles. First they held my hands behind my back and then actually tied them together, gently, then they put a blindfold over my eyes. I later learned that there was a pair of construction paper "sunglasses" taped to this contraption that said "Boy Watcher" on them. How embarrassing! Then I was loaded into a car, which I would later discover to be Laura's Neon, and driven to an undisclosed location. I could tell that Allie was one of the group, as well as LaDonna and Mercedes and a couple others. Laura's little car was packed full!

After they parked, they walked me (still blindfolded) it felt like in circles and up and down steps—all amid a lot of giggling—until finally they seated me and removed the blindfold. We were in Daffys, a restaurant that specializes in lots of noise and birthdays. And Cesar and Jake and Spencer were there too, along with a few others. I think there were about fifteen of us altogether. And what a strange mix we were too. But that just made it all the more memorable and totally cool.

All in all it was a great day. Dad even picked me up after school and took me over to the department of motor vehicles and waited for me to take my driving test (I'd been bugging him for weeks). And amazingly, despite forgetting to adjust my rearview mirror, I passed! Then Dad actually let me drive his BMW all by myself after we got home. I went over and picked up Allie and Laura and we went out for ice cream. Totally cool. And now I am sixteen.

HOW'D I GET HERE?
a year ago all felt lost and hopeless
and a loser times three

i traveled a crooked road
taking one wrong turn after the next
getting more and more lost
and discouraged
then in a moment
in the twinkling of an eye
i became found
and the road i travel
makes sense to me now
most of the time anyway
and when it doesn't
i have a hand to hold onto
and Someone who can lead me
yeah, i'm still not totally sure
just exactly how i got here
but, hey, i'm sure glad i came!
thanks, God!
amen
cm

Sunday, March 9

Thanks to Josh (I owe him big-time) we are not, I repeat not, going off to cruise the Caribbean during spring break. And so our gig at the Samaritan coffeehouse is still on. The reason for this disruption of parental plans is that Josh has decided to go down to Mexico during spring break, to give the orphanage some much needed funding that he and his buddies raised plus a hand with a building project.

Actually, I think it might be some sort of therapy for him as well—to help him mend his broken heart, which I'm pretty sure is quite broken. Anyway, I think Josh promised the parents to do the cruise next year. But fortunately that's a long ways off. And since I was feeling very grateful to my big brother, as well as concerned for my "big sister" Caitlin, I decided to hop on a bus and visit her at school. I hoped that maybe I could cheer her up a little.

And as it turned out, I did. Or at least she said that I did. And I don't think she would lie. She's been pretty down, and I think she needed a little distraction (like me). Anyway, we had a good time, and I got to meet her roommate Liz, who has actually turned out to be a pretty decent sort of person. Okay, she's a little on the cynical side (kind of like I used to be), but I really like her. And I filled Caitlin in on all the latest news about our band and our recent successes and invited her to come to the Samaritan coffeehouse during spring break, which she pretty much promised to do.

So I left feeling like Caitlin is going to be okay. Sure, she seems a little more sober than before. But maybe that's just part of growing up. And I still believe that when the time is right, she and Josh will get back together—and will get

married—<u>happily</u> married. I just think that,
right now, they both (and maybe mostly Josh) have
some more growing up to do. I know that's got to
sound slightly ridiculous coming from the lips
of a sixteen-year-old, but that's the way I see it.
And just for the record, I'm keeping this information strictly between me and my journal and God.

HOW WE GET THERE
we don't know
what lies ahead
that doesn't mean
that we should dread
just hold Your hand
and hold on tight
and You will lead us
through the night
for, God, You know
the way to go
and if we listen
You will show
if we watch
and obey
You will lead us
all the way
cm

Sunday, March 16

We had a woman speak to our church today (a friend of Pastor Tony's). She's from a mission group that works in eastern European countries (like Bulgaria, Romania, Slovakia) by setting up Christian girls' schools. She told about how they provide quality education (not to mention room and board) to girls who've been orphaned and could end up making their living off the streets.

For some reason what this mission group is doing seemed really important to me. I actually cried when she told the story of a thirteen-year-old girl who'd been rescued from prostitution and was now just finishing med school with a brilliant future ahead. And afterward a special offering was taken to help these schools out and all I had was five dollars, which I gave, but I wanted to do something more. I thought about Caitlin and how she got her church involved (in a big way) to reach out to the orphanage in Mexico.

So after church was over and almost everyone was gone or out in the parking lot shooting the breeze, I noticed Pastor Tony joining Steph and the boys over in the back. So I went over and said, "Hi."

"Hey, Chloe," said Steph. "Just the girl I wanted to see. Do you think you'd be able to baby-sit for me after school on Tuesday? I have a dentist appointment."

"Sure."

"Great. How about if I pick you up right at the high school—around three?"

I nodded. "Sounds good. Hey, I have this idea and I wondered if I could toss it out to you guys. It'll only take a minute."

"Sure, what's up?" asked Tony as he picked up Oliver and hoisted him up on his shoulder.

"Well, I really liked what Melinda Bishop said about her missionary group."

"Wasn't that awesome?" said Steph. "What a ministry!"

"Yeah. It's something I feel I could really get behind. Unfortunately, I'm not exactly loaded." I laughed. "But I was thinking about the 'All God's Children' fair we had last year—"

"It's already taking off," said Tony. "Would you like to be involved?"

"Sort of. But maybe in a different way. Do you think my band could do some kind of a benefit concert, at the fair—like just one evening or something—and then we could donate the money to Melinda's ministry?"

"That's a fantastic idea, Chloe."

I smiled. "Yeah, and since we're not so well known, you know, maybe we wouldn't even sell tickets but could just pass around a bucket afterward. If they liked us, maybe they'd chip in."

Tony laughed. "Of course, they'd like you. You girls are terrific. Willy can't say enough about your band. And you took second place in the Battle of the Bands—that says a lot."

"Well, I'll have to talk to Allie and Laura, of course, but I don't know why they'd object. I wish Allie had been at church to hear Melinda today. She had to stay home with her brother."

"She should just bring him with her," said Steph. I'd already told her about David. "He'd do fine in the nursery."

"I'll have to tell her."

"And we have a videotape from Melinda. You could share that with Laura and Allie."

"Cool."

Tony reached over and squeezed my shoulder. "I'm so glad that you're part of this church, Chloe. You really bring a lot with you."

"Thanks."

"And doesn't she remind you of Caitlin?" said Steph with a big smile.

Now I had to laugh at that. "Yeah, Caitlin and me, we look and act so much alike."

"That's not what I mean," said Steph. "I'm talking about what's inside you. You and Caitlin both have these wonderful hearts that really follow God and you both like to help others. I just think that's pretty cool."

"Me too," said Tony.

I nodded. "Thanks."

"Before we go getting all sloppy and mushy," said Tony, "I'll talk to the fair committee about the concert and then let Melinda know about your idea. She might have some informational material or something that we could hand out at the fair."

"And you can pick up that video on Tuesday," suggested Steph.

"I'm hungry," whined Oliver.

"Yeah, I better let you guys get going," I said as I playfully poked Oliver's nose, "before Oliver here starts nibbling on your ear."

He giggled as I started to walk away. "Bye-bye, Chloe!"

Then I walked home from church. I had told my dad this morning that I didn't want a ride since it was such a gorgeous day. On my way home, I decided to stop by the cemetery. I don't even know why. I hadn't been up there for months. But I still remember that rainy day in October when I gave my life to God, and I suppose the graveyard will always be a special place for me. Besides, I was just curious as to how things were going up there.

It was beautiful with emerald green grass and plum trees filled with soft pink blooms and the daffodils—growing with wild abandon all over the place. I picked two sunny blooms and then went over to the old section where I used to spend so much time before. I went straight to Katherine's grave—the one that has the line about dancing with the angels—and laid a daffodil there. Then I went up to Clay's grave—Tony's brother—and laid a daffodil there too.

I sat on the bench and considered just how far I've come in the last six months—like moving from death to life or from A to Z or darkness to light—amazing! Utterly mind-blowing and incredibly, fantastically, totally amazing! And then I lifted my head and my hands, right there in the cemetery, and I sang and praised God. I thanked Him for all that He has done in my past, and for all that He's doing right now, and for all that He will do in my future. For now I know that my future is bright! And I know He loves me! And I know I belong to Him. Amen!

I'M YOURS
i am Yours God
i belong to You
all i am
and all i do
all belongs to You
i am Yours God
my laughter, tears
hope and song
dreams and fears
all belong

to You
i am Yours God
i belong to You
amen
cm

The publisher and author would love to hear your
comments about this book. *Please contact us at:*
www.DOATG.com

THE DIARY OF A TEENAGE GIRL SERIES

ENTER CAITLIN'S WORLD

DIARY OF A TEENAGE GIRL, Caitlin book one

Follow sixteen-year-old Caitlin O'Conner as she makes her way through life—surviving a challenging home life, school pressures, an identity crisis, and the uncertainties of "true love." You'll cry with Caitlin as she experiences heartache, and cheer for her as she encounters a new reality in her life: God. See how rejection by one group can—incredibly—sometimes lead you to discover who you really are.

ISBN 978-1-57673-735-7

IT'S MY LIFE, Caitlin book two

Caitlin faces new trials as she strives to maintain the recent commitments she's made to God. Torn between new spiritual directions and loyalty to Beanie, her pregnant best friend, Caitlin searches out her personal values on friendship, dating, life goals, and family.

ISBN 978-1-59052-053-6

WHO I AM, Caitlin book three

As a high school senior, Caitlin's relationship with Josh takes on a serious tone via e-mail—threatening her commitment to "kiss dating goodbye." When Beanie begins dating an African-American, Caitlin's concern over dating seems to be misread as racism. One thing is obvious: God is at work through this dynamic girl in very real but puzzling ways, and a soul-stretching time of racial reconciliation at school and within her church helps her discover God's will as never before.

ISBN 978-1-59052-890-0

ON MY OWN, Caitlin book four

An avalanche of emotion hits Caitlin as she lands at college and begins to realize she's not in high school anymore. Buried in course-work and far from her best friend, Beanie, Caitlin must cope with her new roommate's bad attitude, manic music, and sleazy social life. Should she have chosen a Bible college like Josh? Maybe...but how to survive the year ahead is the big question right now!

ISBN 978-1-59052-017-8

THE DIARY OF A TEENAGE GIRL SERIES

ENTER CHLOE'S WORLD

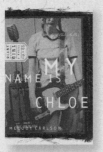

MY NAME IS CHLOE, Chloe book one

Chloe Miller, Josh's younger sister, is a free spirit with dramatic clothes and hair. She struggles with her own identity, classmates, parents, boys, and—whether or not God is for real. But this unconventional high school freshman definitely doesn't hold back when she meets Him in a big, personal way. Chloe expresses God's love and grace through the girl band she forms, Redemption, and continues to show the world she's not willing to conform to anyone else's image of who or what she should be. Except God's, that is.

ISBN 978-1-59052-018-5

SOLD OUT, Chloe book two

Chloe and her fellow band members must sort out their lives as they become a hit in the local community. And after a talent scout from Nashville discovers the trio, all too soon their explosive musical ministry begins to encounter conflicts with family, so-called friends, and school. Exhilarated yet frustrated, Chloe puts her dream in God's hand and prays for Him to work out the details.

ISBN 978-1-59052-141-0

ROAD TRIP, Chloe book three

After signing with a major record company, Redemption's dreams are coming true. Chloe, Allie, and Laura begin their concert tour with the good-looking guys in the band Iron Cross. But as soon as the glitz and glamour wear off, the girls find life on the road a little overwhelming. Even rock solid Laura appears to be feeling the stress—and Chloe isn't quite sure how to confront her about the growing signs of drug addiction...

ISBN 978-1-59052-142-7

FACE THE MUSIC, Chloe book four

Redemption has made it to the bestseller chart, but what Chloe and the girls need most is some downtime to sift through the usual high school stress with grades, friends, guys, and the prom. Chloe struggles to recover from a serious crush on the band leader of Iron Cross. Then just as an unexpected romance catches Redemption by surprise, Caitlin O'Conner—whose relationship with Josh is taking on a new dimension—joins the tour as their chaperone. Chloe's wild ride only speeds up, and this one-of-a-kind musician faces the fact that life may never be normal again.

ISBN 978-1-59052-241-7

Sunday, June 4

Allie and I were just coming out of youth group today when we were practically tackled by Willy. "Did you hear the news?" he asked as he eagerly grabbed us both by the arm. His blue eyes literally flamed with excitement, and a wide smile was splayed across his craggy face. Now to fully appreciate this, you'd have to understand how Willy looks sort of ridiculous when he smiles real big since the tooth next to his front tooth is gold, and his bushy mustache is usually trimmed just slightly crooked.

"What's up, Willy?" I asked. "You look like you

just got a personal message from God or else won the lottery or something."

"Nope. Not me personally. But maybe you guys did."

"What are you talking about?" demanded Allie.

"Well, come in here." He pulled us into Pastor Tony's office. "Okay, sit down, both of you, and take a deep breath. Now listen." He sat in Pastor Tony's big leather chair then leaned forward with his elbows on the desk. "You see," he began slowly, "I have this old friend from the music business, well, he's retired now, but he has a younger friend who's still in the recording industry—and his name is Eric Green, and he's a Christian and is pretty high up in Omega—a Christian recording company. Anyway, I sent him your demo CD a while back and..."

"Cool," said Allie. "Did he like it?"

"Better than that."

"What?" I demanded with a seriously pounding heart. "What in the world are you trying to tell us, Willy?"

"Well..." He actually snickered now. "You have no idea how hard this has been for me, trying not to spill the beans about this whole thing. But Eric called me last weekend and told me he really liked the demo and that he wanted to hear you girls in person, so I told him about the memorial concert, and—"

"A record producer actually came to our concert?" I was standing now, leaning forward and peering at Willy.

He nodded. "And, man, was he ever impressed."

"You're kidding?" Allie stood up too. "A real, honest-to-goodness, legitimate record company?"

He nodded again.

"What does this mean?" I asked, thinking this is just way too good to be true.

"Well, ladies, I think it means he's going to offer Redemption a recording contract."

Allie and I both screamed. We jumped up and down and hugged each other and screamed again, and hugged Willy and thanked him over and over. Then finally after we settled down I begged him to tell us the whole story again—this time with all the details. Then we took some time to call Allie's mom and my parents.

"Have they actually offered you girls a real contract?" my mom asked. The skepticism in her voice was unmistakable.

"No, but Willy thinks there's a pretty good chance they will."

"But are they a reliable company, Chloe? Or are they expecting you girls to invest your own money? I've heard about those companies that tell you you're going to hit the big time, but then they make you pay your own way. It's a real scam. And you know you've already nearly depleted your savings on your little band."

The way she said "little band" was the final blow, but I determined not to let her lack of enthusiasm bring me down. "Oh, I'll explain the details later this afternoon, Mom. Just tell Dad the good news and I'll see you." Parents!

Fortunately, Willy's enthusiasm helped make up for my mom's. And it wasn't Pastor Tony's fault that Allie and I could barely sit still in church. As soon as the service ended, we grabbed Willy and begged him to drive us over to where Laura's church was just getting out. Then you should've heard the three of us girls in Laura's church parking lot. I'm sure half the folks in town heard us squealing.

Finally, Willy hushed us down. "Now, let's not lose our heads just yet because it's still not 100 percent for sure. These things never are, not until the ink from the signatures is dry."

"What's the next step?" asked Laura's dad.

"Yeah," I asked. "What do we do now?"

"Eric wants to fly you girls to Nashville as soon as school is out. You can each bring one parent or guardian. Then you'll do an official audition in the recording studio, and after that the powers that be have a meeting and decide whether they want you or not."

"Do you think we really have a chance?" asked Allie.

"You know, I think we should put this whole

thing into God's hands," said Willy. "Why don't we pray right now?"

And so we did. And to pray like that, out there in the June sunshine, felt like a huge sigh of relief to me. It felt as if the weight was suddenly lifted as we put the whole thing into God's hands. "Your will be done," Willy finally said. And we all said, "Amen!"

Then Willy offered to take Allie and me home and speak with both of our parents. So I waited at Allie's as he explained to Elise what exactly was going on. And it was really sweet to see Allie's little brother Davie climb onto Willy's knee as he spoke. And Davie just sat there quietly playing with Willy's cross (Willy always wears this cross made from two nails hanging by a leather cord) and every once in a while Davie would reach up and pat Willy on the cheek and just smile.

"Well, I guess that sounds legit." Elise stood and shook her head as if it were all just sinking in. "Amazing though. I'm sorry, I don't mean to rush you off, but I really have to be to work in about fifteen minutes."

"No problem." Willy set Davie down on the floor then ruffled his hair.

"And I hope they don't expect me to pay for Allie's plane tickets or hotel room or anything." She frowned as she picked up her work smock and purse. "We're barely scraping by as it is."

He waved his hand. "No, no, you won't need to worry about a thing. The recording company will provide two round-trip tickets as well as food and hotel rooms and any other expenses for each girl along with one adult to accompany her."

Elise looked startled now. "Well, I can't possibly go to Nashville with her. I have work—and I have Davie—and I—"

"Mom!" cried Allie. "You _have_ to go."

"It sounds fun, Allie, but you know as well as I do that it's impossible. I'm sorry, but I don't have time for this right now. We'll just have to figure it out later."

Allie looked slightly disillusioned now, but Willy assured her that it would all work out. "If it's God's will, you don't need to worry about a thing, Allie. It'll all fall right into place."

Next we went to my house, but by the time we got there, my parents had already left. A note on the breakfast bar said they were off playing golf with the Stephensens until four.

"Sorry, Willy," I said as I walked him back to the door.

Willy turned and looked at me. "You should call Josh!"

And so I called and actually got Josh, live, on the phone. He was so excited that he totally made up for Mom's lack of enthusiasm. He whooped and hollered and even told his roommate that his little sister was going to be famous.

And so, despite Mom's ho-hum attitude, I am still excited. I think something big is in the works. And I'm not going to worry because, like Willy said, it's all in God's hands. If He wants it to happen, it will. If not, well, we'll just have to accept that as His will too. But just the same, I really, really want it to happen. I've never felt more alive or more in love with God than that night we did the memorial concert. It's like everything in me was connected that night. It was so right on!

RIGHT ON, GOD
life with You
is so right on
connected
aligned
on target
in sync
together
with-it
bulls-eye
totally jived
right on, God
You are so right on!
amen